"You took me by surprise... You shocked me," she muttered unevenly, struggling to catch her breath.

She was thoroughly unnerved by the sensations that had shimmied up through her taut body and then down again to a place that had ignited with a burst of warmth, mortifying her to the very bone.

Enzo released his breath on a measured hiss. "Relax. For a moment, I was tempted. But nothing is going to happen unless you want it to. I'm attracted to you. I know I shouldn't be but I'm not perfect. In fact, it seems I'm all too human. But you are completely safe with me, *piccolo mio.*"

"Maybe I don't need to be safe...with you," Skye said uncertainly. "You make me feel things I didn't expect to feel. You make me curious. I know, like you said, I shouldn't be in these circumstances. But the truth is, I am and I'm attracted too."

"So..." Enzo breathed a touch raggedly. "What do you want to do about this?"

"We—we could try a kiss...just *one*," she stressed.

Cinderella Sisters for Billionaires

Once upon a time...Cinderella met a billionaire!

There is one thing that the Davison sisters know all too well: life *isn't* a fairy tale! Until their ordinary lives are made extraordinary...by the arrival of two billionaires. But while it feels like the start of two love stories for the ages, will the Cinderella sisters live happily ever after?

Find out in...
Enzo and Skye's story
The Maid Married to the Billionaire
Available now!

And look out for
The Maid's Pregnancy Bombshell
Coming soon!

Lynne Graham

THE MAID MARRIED TO THE BILLIONAIRE

HARLEQUIN
PRESENTS

Recycling programs for this product may not exist in your area.

ISBN-13: 978-1-335-59270-5

The Maid Married to the Billionaire

Copyright © 2023 by Lynne Graham

For questions and comments about the quality of this book, please contact us at CustomerService@Harlequin.com.

Harlequin Enterprises ULC
22 Adelaide St. West, 41st Floor
Toronto, Ontario M5H 4E3, Canada
www.Harlequin.com

Printed in U.S.A.

Lynne Graham was born in Northern Ireland and has been a keen romance reader since her teens. She is very happily married to an understanding husband who has learned to cook since she started to write! Her five children keep her on her toes. She has a very large dog who knocks everything over, a very small terrier who barks a lot and two cats. When time allows, Lynne is a keen gardener.

Books by Lynne Graham

Harlequin Presents

The Ring the Spaniard Gave Her
The Italian's Bride Worth Billions
The Baby the Desert King Must Claim

Heirs for Royal Brothers

Cinderella's Desert Baby Bombshell
Her Best Kept Royal Secret

The Stefanos Legacy

Promoted to the Greek's Wife
The Heirs His Housekeeper Carried
The King's Christmas Heir

Visit the Author Profile page
at Harlequin.com for more titles.

CHAPTER ONE

A LARGE AND expensive four-by-four awaited Lorenzo Durante when he arrived in his private jet at Norwich airport.

It had been a long time since he had driven himself. Limousines were more Enzo's style. He gritted his teeth. He didn't whine about stuff, and he wasn't a kid any more. He had got himself into his current predicament and he would get himself out of it again. That he was unlikely to enjoy the experience of relinquishing his affluent way of life went without saying but then wasn't that part of the punishment?

His grandfather, Eduardo Martelli, had, however, insisted that the challenge he had set *wasn't* a punishment. Eduardo had preached at length about the need for Enzo to *grow up*. Just remembering that demeaning phrase made Enzo seethe, his quick, hot temper ready to spark. He compressed his lips, his lean, darkly handsome features taut. He was twenty-seven years old and aside from his university studies and spells as an intern, he had never worked a day in his life. Why would he have? Orphaned as a baby, he had inherited billions from his late father, Narciso.

His maternal grandparents were nowhere near as wealthy as his paternal grandparents had been, yet they had fought them for custody and, probably because they were younger and healthier than their opponents, had won the case. In court they had promised to raise their grandson in what they had termed an *ordinary* life. Sadly, they had had their work cut out on that front, Enzo acknowledged ruefully, thinking of the legion of Durante relations and hangers-on who had constantly invaded his childhood with their visits and invitations, their ridiculously lavish gifts and their eagerness to tempt him into the supremely privileged permissive lifestyle his late father had enjoyed.

Somewhere around his twenty-third birthday, after he had completed his education in the business world, he mused grimly, the seduction had begun to work. Fresh from university and nursing a broken heart, Enzo had been vulnerable to the temptation of the playboy lifestyle. That was where it had started, the slow steady sink into a self-indulgent decadence that had appalled the grandparents who in every way had truly been his parents.

And a few years on, the inevitable had happened: his two lifestyles had collided and fatally clashed. The scandalous headlines their grandson attracted had been studiously ignored by Eduardo and Sophie Martelli. But after he had made the fatal mistake of attending a social occasion drunk with an equally drunken partner, the balloon had gone up on forgiveness. He still broke out in a cold sweat when he recalled that evening. The next day he had attempted to apologise. Eduardo Martelli had refused to listen while his wife had simply sobbed in embarrassment and heartbreak because her husband seemed determined to disown the grandson she adored.

That had been the shocking moment when Enzo had realised that it didn't matter how much money he had, how many friends or what exciting opportunities to enjoy himself still shone on his horizon. He had finally appreciated how much more his family meant to him and his loving grandmother's distress had shamed him. And coming to England, taking charge of a small company recently acquired by his grandfather and striving to live a more *useful*, normal life was the price of reconciliation. Only there was nothing normal about it, Enzo conceded in exasperation, not on *his* terms.

He drew up at the house he was to use. It was in the back of beyond, a couple of miles from the nearest town and larger than he had expected. He was accustomed to spacious accommodation, but a serviced apartment would have suited him better than an old country house with a turret. He hoped it looked better inside than it did from the outside.

Minutes later, Enzo contemplated the fresh horror of an antique furnished décor and an empty kitchen, when he was starving. How the hell was he supposed to manage alone when he couldn't cook? First world problem, he lamented wryly, and probably the opening to a long line of such jarring wake-up calls. He would manage, of course he would.

An hour later, the takeaway pizza he had ordered thrust into the bin in disgust, Enzo drove into the town to find a restaurant. He couldn't find one. He located a twenty-four-hour supermarket but drove past it, deciding that he could do without eating for one night. Instead, he went to check out the business he would be dragging into the twenty-first century. The office block beside the factory he had to overhaul was substantial. He would be as popular as poison when he arrived in the morning as the new CEO. It had been a family business and there would be redundancies, restructuring, all the changes necessary to make the firm viable again.

On his drive back to the house he drove past a car parked by the side of the road, a young woman standing by its bonnet. A woman on her own in the dark with a broken-down car. A groan of frustration escaped him. He didn't want to get involved. Nobody would ever accuse Enzo of being a good Samaritan, but he was too well brought up to ignore the dangers threatening a woman in such a situation. Bit-ing back a curse of irritation, he turned the car and drove back, buzzing down the window to lean out…

One hour earlier

Skye lay where she fell after Ritchie threw her viciously away from him. She was so terrified she couldn't breathe, wasn't even sure a breath could manage to squeeze past her agonisingly sore throat. He had semi-strangled her but only after he had first punched her in the face and the stomach to bring her down, glaring down at her like a madman as though he hated her, and then kicking her. She felt as if she was broken inside, as though the world had stopped suddenly and flung her off at a height and she was still falling. Shock was roaring through her because Ritchie had never hit her before. He had shouted but there had never been any violence.

Ritchie was still ranting, crashing about the bedroom, slamming doors, shouting abuse back at her. She stayed still, eyes shut tight, afraid he would notice her again, *hurt* her again. Or worse, get so mad at her lack of response that he hurt the children. Brodie, the poor little mite, having seen the attack, had rushed in front of her in a pathetic toddler attempt to protect her but she had managed to get between him and Ritchie and get Brodie into the safety of his bedroom. Her frantic intervention had only made Ritchie angrier than ever. She needed to get herself and the kids out of the apartment fast but Ritchie would never willingly let her leave him. She stayed on the floor, quiet as a mouse, her heart thumping at an insane rate as she played dead.

'You stupid cow! I'm going down to the off-licence!' Ritchie spat down at her.

A moment later, the front door slammed and she was up, trying to move at speed but then staggering in pain, groaning helplessly at the burning agony of her battered ribs. She stumbled straight into the kids' room, found her little brother, Brodie, sobbing and frightened on his bed, and she reached for him first.

'We're going out,' she told him soothingly, smoothing his tumbled blond curls. 'But you have to be quiet.'

She scooped her sleeping sister, Shona, straight out of her cot, snatching up a cot blanket to keep the baby extra warm. Her feet were bare and she looked in vain for her shoes. Brodie was clingy and anxious, which was hardly surprising after what he had witnessed. It was bad enough that Ritchie had attacked her but unimaginable that she could have allowed him to hurt a two-year-old in his ungovernable rage.

It was *her* fault, she thought in an agony of guilt. After all, she had chosen to move in with Ritchie. She was the fool who had put her innocent siblings into contact with such a man and put them at risk. But she hadn't known, hadn't dreamt what Ritchie might be capable of in a temper. And now that she knew, now that she had learned her mistake, she was leaving. But there was no time to pack. There was too big a risk of Ritchie coming back before she could get away. She could return for their stuff later when everything had calmed down and he was hopefully at work.

Hands all clumsy fingers and thumbs, she strapped the kids into their car seats and collapsed into the driver's seat, saying a momentary prayer to the god of ancient motor vehicles that Mavis would start for her because Mavis, her late mother's elderly car, could be very temperamental. When the engine burst into noisy life, she heaved a sigh of relief and moved off, hunched over the wheel while she worried about where on earth she would go. A homeless shelter? A women's refuge? Hopefully there would be somewhere in the town that would take them in. If not, they would have to spend the night in the car. Escaping Ritchie would be only the first step on a stony road, she conceded unhappily, guilt pulling at her afresh.

Enzo leant out of the window of his car.

'Do you need help?'

'Do you know anything about cars?' Skye asked hopefully.

Suppressing a sigh, Enzo climbed out. He had spent his teens tinkering with engines. Unfortunately, one glance under the rusted bonnet was sufficient to tell him that it had been at least a decade since even basic maintenance had been carried out on the old banger. 'It could be any one of a number of problems,' he pointed out wryly. 'Have you called anyone? Do you belong to a motoring organisation?'

'I'm afraid not and I haven't called anyone, but I don't have anyone I can call, right now,' she framed awkwardly, stepping back from him because he was very tall and broad and somehow elegantly intimidating, beautifully dressed as he was in a business suit.

Enzo looked at her for the first time. She had blonde corkscrew curls that fluffed round her triangular features like a tousled lion's mane *and...*there was something wrong with her face. If she would just move out of the shadows into the brightness of his headlights, he could get a better look at her.

'There must be someone,' Enzo told her confidently. 'Friends? A family member?'

'No, at this time of night there's really no one,' she insisted uncomfortably, stepping off one foot onto the other.

Enzo stilled and scrutinised her bare feet in disbelief. 'Why do you have no shoes on? It's freezing tonight!'

'I left home in a hurry.' She tried to laugh but the effort seemed to choke her. Her hand flew up to her face and she winced in obvious pain.

'You're hurt,' Enzo registered in consternation. 'Was there an accident? Should I call the police?'

'No, please don't get the police,' she urged with a shiver of dismay.

'Then what can I do to help you?'

'Just drive on. You did the kind thing and stopped but I'm not really in a position to *be* helped, unless you can fix the car,' she muttered shakily.

'I can't leave you out here on your own,' Enzo objected, peering down at her as she shifted position. She was very small, possibly about five feet tall and probably only about a hundred pounds soaking wet as well as being pretty young. 'Surely I can drop you off somewhere?'

As she moved forward, he saw her swollen face, the partially closed eye and the ring of dark bluish bruising circling her throat like a macabre necklace. '*Madonna mia*, you've been attacked and you're hurt! Is that why you left home in such a hurry?'

'Yeah, we're running away, just not doing a very efficient job of it,' she mumbled shakily.

'I'll ring a breakdown company,' Enzo informed her, digging out his phone, only vaguely wondering why she had referred to 'we' when she was alone.

'I'm not sure I can afford one.'

'Then let it be at my expense,' Enzo urged, searching for the nearest breakdown service on his phone, keen to find a solution and move them on. 'But let me take you to the nearest hospital now. You need medical attention.'

'Do I look that bad?' she asked baldly.

'You look like someone tried to strangle you and you got punched in the face,' Enzo bit out in a taut undertone, for although he knew that some men beat up women he had never come across it in his own life and he was very much shocked by the state she was in. 'A doctor should look at you, but I still believe that the police would be the best option as a first port of call.'

'I *can't* go to the police.'

Enzo lowered his phone with a frown of irritation. 'Your car can't be picked up until tomorrow. I'll drive you into town.'

'I don't know you… I can't get into a car with you!' Skye gasped.

'My name is Lorenzo Durante. My friends call me Enzo. And you are…?'

'Skye Davison,' she provided reluctantly.

'If I leave you here,' Enzo murmured drily, 'I'll be informing the police of your location and the condition I found you in.'

'Why on earth would you do that?' Skye gasped.

'In case something happens to you, or the driver of one of the cars that have already been past assumes that I'm responsible for your condition!' he completed grimly.

'Oh, for goodness' sake!' Skye exclaimed, out of all patience.

'I have a solution. One of my employees is a qualified paramedic,' he told her. 'If you were agreeable,

Paola could check you out at my home but, firstly, let's get you some shoes.'

'Paola…is that a woman's name?'

Enzo nodded confirmation and saw some of her tension evaporate because she found the mention of another woman reassuring.

'But first we'll get you a pair of shoes,' he repeated stubbornly, evidently finding her shoeless state intolerable.

Skye caved in. 'I'll have to move the car seats over…and I hope you don't mind dogs.'

Enzo frowned in bewilderment as she moved round to open the passenger door. 'Car seats? You have a dog?'

Over her shoulder inside the dim interior of the old car, he glimpsed a baby covered to the chin by a blanket and beyond her a dozing toddler. Something small and wriggly bounced out of the passenger seat foot well to dance round his feet.

'That's Sparky,' she said hoarsely, detaching the straps holding the baby and lifting the baby to settle her down in the foot well while she removed the car seat.

As another's car's headlights lit up the night, Enzo bent down and scooped up the little dachshund and put him straight into his car before he could streak off and become roadkill. As Skye struggled to lift the baby's car seat, he lifted it out of her arms and settled it into the back seat. Registering that she was in too much pain to bend and do what had to be done, he reached in and took care of it, reaching out for the baby and tucking it into the cosy carrier to snap the belt closed again.

'Thanks,' she said in surprise that he should have done that for her, for Ritchie had never helped with the children.

The little boy started crying the minute he saw Enzo. 'It's not your fault.' Skye sighed. 'He's just a bit scared of men after what he saw tonight—'

'The assault happened in front of him?' Enzo exclaimed as she lifted out the toddler, leaving him free to remove the second car seat.

'I'm afraid so. I feel so guilty about it,' she whispered.

'You don't have anything to feel guilty about,' Enzo told her squarely. 'It's not your fault that you were attacked.'

Enzo attached the second seat and helped her to stow the little boy into it. All that finally accomplished, he closed the door on his unexpected cargo. Two children and a dog, he was thinking in sheer wonderment. But what else could he do but help? It was an emergency.

The transfer complete, Skye clambered painfully and slowly up into the front passenger seat. 'I'm so sorry about all this,' she mumbled. 'I'm sure you don't need the hassle.'

'Takes my mind off my own problems,' he countered calmly. 'I'll ring Paola while you're in the supermarket buying some shoes.'

His complete calm and assurance were wonderfully soothing to her raw nerves.

'Will you stay in the car with the children?' she heard herself ask daringly.

'I'm not going to abandon them and we don't want to move them again at this time of night,' he pointed out.

A few minutes later, he drew up in the car park and said, 'Would you like me to go in first and get shoes for you?'

Skye shook her head and that hurt too. She didn't think there was a single part of her body free from aches and pains. 'No, I'll be fine.'

Relieved she had brought her bag, she went into the shop, receiving barely a glance from the security guard on the door. She grabbed a basket and selected a pair of canvas shoes from the display, hurrying round to the baby section to pick up nappies, baby milk and a bottle and a few other necessities for her siblings, grateful that she had enough money from a recent tax refund to cover her purchases and keeping her head down to avoid notice.

When she returned to the car, Enzo was on the phone talking in another language. He had rung Paola at the hotel his security team were using and asked the older woman to meet him at the house. She complained vehemently about the fact he had gone out again without his bodyguards. In return, he told her about Skye and the children. She wanted to know why Skye wasn't willing to go to the police. Enzo admitted that he had no idea and had hesitated to push lest she took fright. He had thought it was more important to help her than demand answers about what was, strictly speaking, none of his business.

'Paola will meet us at my home,' he advanced, finishing the call. 'If you can give me ten minutes I'll go and buy coffee and a few essentials because there's no food in the house.'

'Why not?' she asked as he swung out and the lights from the shop illuminated him.

Her breath caught in her throat as she saw him clearly for the first time. He was exceptionally handsome with sculpted cheekbones, a strong hard jawline and dark deep-set eyes set below straight ebony brows. His hair was black and thick, cropped short. His whole vibe was stylish and classy from his haircut to the fashionable cut of his fancy suit.

'I only arrived at the house this evening. I haven't had time to get anything in.'

'I can do without coffee,' she told him.

Enzo raised a perfect dark brow. 'I *can't*.'

And then he was gone, the stranger who was being kind to her when the man she had believed she loved and who loved her had almost killed her. There was a lesson there somewhere and inevitably the inescapable fact that she needed to cut Ritchie out of her life.

Not that she had any doubts about doing that, especially not after what he had done to her.

Enzo returned with a couple of carrier bags and drove off again. 'The house isn't far. Paola will tell you if she thinks you need to go to hospital.'

'How could I go to a hospital with the kids in tow?' she asked ruefully.

'You must have been very young when you had them,' Enzo remarked.

'They're not mine. They're my brother and sister,' she confided. 'My mother and stepfather died in a train derailment almost a year ago. Shona was only a month old.'

The strangest pang of relief that the baby and the toddler were not hers trickled through Enzo and he questioned it, wondering why he should even have an opinion about such a thing. 'I'm sorry for your loss.'

'Thank you but, in an odd way, the kids saved my younger sister Alana and I from falling apart at the seams. We had to keep going for their sake.'

'Were you running away from a husband tonight?' he asked flatly.

'No, a boyfriend. Luckily, we're not married,' she whispered. 'And although splitting up poses some challenges, we don't own property together or anything else.'

Enzo filtered the car off the road and down a driveway lined with tall laurel hedges.

Her jaw dropped when she saw the big Victorian

house with the spectacular tower attached to one end. '*This* is where you live?' she queried.

'As of this evening, yes,' Enzo confirmed without enthusiasm. 'Paola is already here. I suppose we'll have to bring the kids and the dog indoors too.'

'Yes. You wouldn't want to see what Brodie could get up to left in a car by himself.'

His head of security awaited them in the front porch. Her eyes widened into a fixed stare when she saw Enzo with Brodie in his arms. The toddler was grizzling and cross and wriggling like a snake in a sack.

'Let's get inside first,' he suggested as Paola led the way into the gracious hall.

'I'll check Skye over in the sitting room,' Paola announced, her first-aid bag firmly gripped in her hand. 'Are you able to look after the children?'

Brodie sobbed into his shoulder and tried to struggle free. 'I'll manage,' Enzo intoned with determination.

As he set the toddler down on his own feet rather than risk dropping him, Skye handed him the baby. 'Try not to wake her up,' she advised.

Enzo walked into the kitchen and sat down, heaving a sigh. Rescuing women was exhausting and frustrating and he lacked the appropriate skill set required for tending to children, but he knew that he still would have helped Skye even had he known that she had children and a dog in the car with her.

'Who you?' Brodie demanded tearfully, stopping dead in front of Enzo, stretching up, striving to look bigger than he was.

'I'm Enzo.'

'I'm hungry,' Brodie announced. 'And I have to go potty.'

Enzo almost groaned out loud, suddenly grateful that he had noticed where the downstairs cloakroom was and leading the little boy there.

'I need help,' Brodie told him.

Clutching the baby under one arm and thinking that it was really a remarkably accommodating baby, Enzo crouched down to help Brodie with his clothes. That accomplished, he turned on the tap for the toddler to wash his hands. He couldn't believe what a production it was to take care of so simple a task.

'The boss doesn't know anything about children.' Paola was chuckling as she attended to Skye in the elegant drawing room. 'It'll be an education for him.'

'He's been very kind to us,' Syke said ruefully. 'But when he saw the kids and the dog I think he was tempted to run. Don't tell him I said that but his face was a study. Is he single?'

'Very much so, not the settling-down type,' the older woman confirmed calmly. 'I think your ribs are bruised rather than cracked so you'll just have to nurse them along until they heal. Your throat, try not to talk too much and rest it. That's more serious and I still think you should have let the boss take you to hospital.'

'The nearest hospital is miles away and the children have gone through enough tonight.'

'You need to go to the police and report the assault.'

Skye looked away uncomfortably. 'I *can't*.'

'Why not? He might do this again and you might not survive the next time.'

Skye paled and winced. 'He's in the police. How could I report him where he works? They might not even believe me and he's bound to have friends there and then he would find out where I am. I think he has a tracker app on my phone.'

Paola studied her, appalled. 'He's a policeman? You *still* have to report him. As for the app, give me your phone now and I'll check it. If there's an app, I'll remove it.'

Skye walked back out into the hall and saw Enzo with Brodie at his feet and a still slumbering Shona draped over one broad shoulder. She hovered uncomfortably while Paola took her leave and departed through the front door, having returned her phone to her.

'I should get going as well,' Skye remarked.

'That would be crazy this late at night when I have at least six bedrooms empty here,' Enzo contended. 'Pick your own rooms upstairs.'

Skye winced. 'That's very generous of you *but—*'

Enzo surveyed her lazily. Without the bruising and swelling that marred her delicate features, he surmised, she would be very pretty. 'No, I'm being practical and you need to try and see the bigger picture here. You and the children are *safe* under this roof. I have twenty-four-seven security. You can also lock yourself into your room. You will not be disturbed, I assure you. You are totally free to leave the house any time you wish.'

Skye reddened and checked the time, lifting Shona off his shoulder with an exhausted sigh of surrender. He crouched down to lift Brodie, who was mumbling in a semi-doze. 'I'll show you upstairs. I'll be leaving early in the morning for work. If you want a lift into town, let me know.'

One of the bedrooms had a cot as well as a bed and Skye immediately opted for that room because she could share the bed with Brodie. Mercifully the bed was already made up and she lowered the side of the cot to slide her little sister in, covering her with her blanket.

'If you hadn't run into me, where were you planning to go tonight?' Enzo asked from the doorway.

'There's a homeless shelter in town but that would involve social services and I'm worried that they would take the kids into care.'

'Are you their legal guardian?'

'Yes, but when that was agreed, I was living with

my sister and working as a teacher. My life was... stable. Now everything's changed.'

'A teacher? What age group?'

'Kindergarten but my first job was only temporary, and when my sister got a live-in job at the hotel, I couldn't afford the rent of our apartment on my own. Ritchie asked me to move in with him and agreeing has to be the worst decision I ever made. For a start he didn't want me to find another job. I should have smelt a rat then,' she confided tightly. 'And now here I am, homeless, unemployed and practically penniless.'

'You'll get through,' Enzo assured her. 'Now let's both get some sleep.'

'Thanks for everything,' she muttered as he turned away.

'Think of it as my good deed for the day,' Enzo commented lightly. 'And I haven't done so many that I deserve your gratitude. I'm a selfish bastard at the best of times.'

'You weren't tonight when it mattered,' Skye responded.

Closing the door, she turned the key in the lock. Yes, she felt better in a securely locked room now, she conceded uncomfortably. It would be a long time, if ever, before she relaxed around a man again.

She undressed her little brother and tucked him into bed, walking through to the old-fashioned bathroom to stare in horror at her reflection. Paola had given her painkillers and if she didn't try to move too fast the pain was now a dulled ache but, unfortunately, she was aching all over, in fact even her face ached. Tomorrow she would have a multicoloured black eye.

And she still had to get their possessions collected. How was she supposed to do that without a car? She probably didn't even have the money to pay for the necessary repairs to get her car back! Recognising that her worries were rising in an ever-increasing spiral of woe, she calmed herself. She would deal with each problem as it came up and resolve it. She had to be strong and steady, only dealing with one problem at a time.

It was painful to recall how much she had trusted Ritchie. He had asked her to marry him and, secure in that proposal of his, she had surrendered pretty much all her freedom, believing that he would offer her and her siblings a better life. So, she had ignored his lack of enthusiasm for the amount of time she spent with her siblings, his jealous and sulky behaviour if another man so much as looked at her, his eagerness to determine where she went and who she spoke to, not to mention his need to know where she was virtually every hour of the day. Yes, she had ignored, overlooked or forgiven far too much, believing that he loved her and was simply insecure.

Alana, on the other hand, had never liked Ritchie, deeming him too possessive. Skye had believed she loved him, although now she knew it hadn't been real love because she was painfully aware that she didn't ever want to lay eyes on him again. But she had loved him for accepting the children with her, loved him for seemingly seeing her as special when nobody had ever seen her in that light before. And it had all been an illusion, wishful thinking more than fact, because she had thought he loved her too.

After a shower, Enzo slid into bed and made plans. He would offer Skye a job as his housekeeper. He wouldn't be at the house much because he would be working long hours but, when he was here, he wanted to be comfortable. And he wouldn't be comfortable if he had to worry about shopping and learning to cook and all that jazz. That short supermarket visit, the first of his entire life, had been an unnerving experience. Surprisingly he didn't really mind the kids once he had got used to their unpredictability, although that baby would sleep through a riot, he conceded in admiration. In any case, it was a big enough house to lose two kids and a dog in, he reflected thankfully.

It had never occurred to him that he might actually like children. After his disastrous experience of love at university had taught him how little some women could be trusted, he had assumed that he would never marry and never have children of his own. Only now did it strike him that he shouldn't allow that experience to dictate the rest of his life.

Skye woke up as usual when Shona let out a hungry wail. She felt like wailing too because she was also hungry and thirsty. Her sudden movement to get out of bed reminded her sharply of her condition. A jagged moan of pain was wrenched from her and Brodie sat up with a start.

'Bekfast,' he said cheerfully, unconcerned by their unfamiliar surroundings.

She had a quick shower in the bathroom, took care of her siblings and was about to go downstairs with them when a knock sounded on the door. She undid the lock and peered out through the gap.

'I heard the children and thought you might appreciate a change of clothes.' Enzo extended a pile of clothing. 'It's not much and we're a hopeless mismatch in size but it's better than nothing.'

'Thank you,' Skye said. 'That was thoughtful of you.'

Brodie squeezed past her. 'Enzo!' her little brother carolled in delight as though Enzo were his best pal.

'I'll be down in two minutes,' she called, shaking out a T-shirt and a pair of sweats.

She shed her jeans and sweater, dispensed with her underwear and pulled on the T-shirt. She rolled up the legs on the sweat pants and pulled the ties at the waist tight to keep them up on her slender frame.

She looked ridiculous but feeling clean made her feel immensely better.

Enzo took her breath away in his conservative navy pinstripe suit teamed with a dark shirt and red silk tie. He was standing with the microwave oven open.

'S'not a toaster,' Brodie was saying authoritatively.

'It may have a toasting mechanism,' Enzo told the little boy very seriously.

'I'll take care of the toast,' Skye said with amusement, Shona clasped under one arm while she filled the kettle to make a bottle for the baby. 'I need the baby stuff I left behind.'

'I'll send you over with a car and a driver today and you can collect it all. I also have a proposition to make,' Enzo announced. 'I need a housekeeper. You need a job and a roof over your head. Interested?'

CHAPTER TWO

S<small>KYE FROWNED IN</small> surprise and then nodded as she filled the bottle and mixed it before plunging it into cold water to cool. 'I could be. Where's Sparky?'

'Out in the back garden. I'm afraid we've no food for him,' Enzo reminded her.

'Sparky hungie… Brodie hungie,' her little brother complained.

'Hungry,' she corrected as she slotted bread into the toaster. 'The toast is on now and I bought some cereal last night.'

Housekeeping, she reflected absently. It would give them a safe place to live and allow her to continue looking after the children. Taking care of one man's household requirements didn't sound too onerous either and, best of all, while she was earning she would be free to search out another teaching job, temporary or otherwise. Allowing Ritchie to clip her employment wings and keep her at home had been a mistake but at the time she had been glad of the opportunity to spend time with her newly bereaved little brother and sister. It had been a period of terrible upheaval for all of them, she conceded belatedly. Maybe grief for the loving parents she had lost had played a part in her decision to move in with Ritchie.

'Let me take the baby,' Enzo offered, reaching out to cradle Shona and sit down by the kitchen table.

'Exactly what would the job entail?' Skye asked.

'It would only be for a couple of months because I won't be in England much beyond Christmas,' Enzo warned. 'You look after the house and the shopping and the cooking and I'll be happy. I only need a late evening meal. I'll be working most of the time.'

Skye tested the milk from the bottle on her wrist. 'It sounds good. I could do with some breathing space to get myself back together before I make a fresh start somewhere. What would you pay me?'

Enzo quoted a sum.

'That's far too much!' she told him instantly, shocked by the amount of money he was offering her.

'You'll be doing everything here and I suspect that you could do with the money,' Enzo pointed out calmly. 'As soon as your car is back on the road, you'll have your independence back.'

'I'll take it. What's the address of this place? I need to let my sister know where we are.'

Taking note of the address, she gathered Shona back into her arms, and gave her the bottle, which she drank happily, big blue eyes firmly locked on Skye's face.

'If you can get the coffee machine to produce a decent coffee, there'll be a bonus,' Enzo informed her wryly.

'It's not rocket science.'

'Might as well be.' Enzo sighed, watching her pour cereal for Brodie and seat him at the table before starting to butter toast. 'You're good at multitasking.'

'You have to be with kids. Do you want any toast?' she asked.

Her slight frame was really tiny in his clothes and there was something oddly sexy about knowing she was wearing something of his against her skin. He didn't know what it was, didn't wish to dwell on that angle. Such considerations were out of bounds now that she was an employee. In any case, he was very aware of how vulnerable she was right now; she'd clearly been in an abusive relationship and he felt a responsibility towards her. He would need to be careful to make her feel safe and not give her any reason to be nervous around him.

Her movements were very stiff and he noticed that she was avoiding bending or twisting as best she could, not an easy challenge with young children to look after, he reflected grimly. One eye was encircled with multicoloured bruising but nothing could hide her delicate bone structure, her pale-as-alabaster, perfect skin or the soft fullness of her pink lips.

'Enzo? *Toast?*' she queried when he failed to respond.

Enzo shook his handsome dark head a little as though to clear his thoughts. 'No, thanks. I like fruit, coffee and a croissant in the morning.'

'OK, you've got yourself a housekeeper,' Skye told him. 'I'll get our stuff picked up today and go shopping.'

He set a black credit card down on the table.

'What's my budget?'

'There isn't one.'

'What do you like to eat?' Skye enquired as she dug a small notebook out of her bag and flashed a pen. 'And what do you *not* like?'

Those details acquired, Enzo stood up. 'We have to exchange phone numbers. I'm sending two men with you to collect your belongings just in case your ex is there and causes trouble. You need to be protected and you will have the kids with you, which is enough of a challenge.'

'Thanks. I'm very grateful. Could you take the car seats out of your car before you leave?' Skye reminded him as she took his number and shot a text to him.

In truth, she was dreading that moment that she would have to enter the apartment, unsure as to Ritchie's whereabouts. Stalwart male company would be a very welcome support.

As it was still early, she decided to ring her sister and hope to catch her before she went to bed. Alana worked a permanent night shift at the hotel where she worked and lived and usually slept in the mornings but there would have been no point in calling Alana the night before because she didn't have a car, she had a bicycle, and, in any case, would have been at work. Skye still needed Alana's help though and she had to tell her what had happened and that Ritchie was out of her life now. Her sibling often spent the afternoons with her and the children and she wanted Alana to know that she was no longer at the apartment. The last thing she wanted to risk was her sister running into Ritchie without knowing how volatile the situation with him was.

Alana came on the phone on a bright, breezy note. 'It's my day off…well, at least until I report for duty tonight again. My co-worker called in sick.' She sighed before she listened in disgust to what her sister had to tell her and she immediately offered to take care of the children while Skye removed her possessions from Ritchie's apartment.

Skye had dressed the kids, fed poor Sparky some toast and cleaned up the kitchen by the time the two men, Matteo and Antonio, arrived. Alana arrived soon after them.

'Oh, my word, your face!' Alana gasped in horror when she saw her sibling's black eye.

Alana was the taller, curvier version of Skye with blonde hair, gloriously *straight* blonde hair that Skye envied, down to her waist. 'I should kill Ritchie for what he's done to you!' her kid sister swore fiercely.

Skye calmed her down and left her with the children, grateful for her sister's support. She felt like a tramp in Enzo's overly large clothes with the ugly bruises marring her face and decided she would live in her sunglasses for the next week. Her nervous tension climbed as the car was parked outside the small apartment block.

The apartment was mercifully empty. Feeling as though she were in some television competition for speed or a supermarket trolley rush, Skye clasped a roll of binbags and went into the children's room first.

In the midst of dismantling Shona's cot and recalling that there were a baby buggy, a high chair and various other bulky equipment as well, she noticed Antonio was on the phone. 'We'll need a van to move all of it,' he explained as Skye rammed clothes into a bag. 'But Matteo will arrange one for us.'

'I should've said there was so much large stuff before we came.' Skye sighed guiltily while Antonio bagged toys for her, leaving her free to go into the bedroom she had briefly shared with Ritchie.

She grimaced as she glanced at the bed, averting her gaze from a place she had begun to dread. No, she didn't like sex. Contrary to every article she read, she hadn't enjoyed it. That might put her in a minority but that was just how she was and, now that Ritchie was out of her life again, she could be honest about the fact. All that faking and pretending an enjoyment she didn't feel to keep Ritchie happy had drained her, made her feel dishonest and, what was more, a little on the odd side because she evidently didn't like what other women liked. Well, that was done and dusted now, she reminded herself. A man-free future stretched in front of her.

Skye had had such great hopes when she'd moved in with Ritchie and it hurt her pride to remember her trusting naivety. She lifted the photograph of her mother and stepfather from the bedside cabinet and tears of grief stung her eyes. Their loving happiness together had become her ideal and it seemed laughable now to recall that she had actually hoped to build the same kind of relationship with Ritchie. After all, her stepfather had taken on two little girls that weren't his own and treated them as though they were his own flesh and blood.

Ritchie's readiness to accept that she came as a package with Brodie and Shona had encouraged her to believe that he was a man similar to her stepfather. But once she had moved in with Ritchie, he had had little time to spare for her siblings and he had complained bitterly that the children were always underfoot. He had also accused her of always putting her siblings first.

In reality, she had done the opposite and she was ashamed of that fact. She had put herself first. She had grabbed at that whole fantasy dream of a supportive, caring partner who would lighten her load and make her feel less alone, but family life had been too restrictive and domestic for Ritchie. For all his talk of marriage, he hadn't been ready to settle down. He might've wanted her, but the children had just been unfortunate baggage that came along with her.

She finished putting her clothes and shoes into bags and hauled them out to the lounge, ready for the van that was coming. She pounced with relief on her sunglasses and put them on.

The two men concentrated on getting her belongings down in the lift and packing the car. While she was helping them move the baby equipment down to the ground floor, the van arrived and, with it, another man, who made short work of loading everything. She was smiling as she walked out of the apartment block and was totally disconcerted to find herself unexpectedly confronted by Ritchie.

'Where the hell have you been?' he demanded wrathfully as he strode up onto the pavement. 'You were out all night and you didn't phone. I was worried sick about you!'

Skye froze where she stood. Surprisingly, Ritchie looked the same as always. Blond hair, an aggres-

sively square jaw, pale blue eyes, an angry flush
on his cheeks. He wasn't in uniform, clearly wasn't
working and she realised with an inner shiver that
they had been very lucky that he hadn't come home
while they were still in the apartment. At least she
had got all their stuff out without any hassle, although she had left behind kitchen equipment and
china she had brought from her own home because
she couldn't afford storage costs and could hardly
clutter up Enzo's imposing house with her household goods.

'I asked you a question!' Ritchie reminded her,
towering over her menacingly and glowering at Antonio. 'And who is this man?'

'I'm moving out, Ritchie,' Skye framed tautly.
'This is the last time you'll see me.'

'Back away,' Antonio told Ritchie, stretching a
protective arm out in front of Skye. 'You're getting
too close.'

'What the hell are you playing at, Skye?' Ritchie
demanded furiously. 'Why would you move out? So,
we had a little fallout…'

Syke whipped off her sunglasses. 'You call this a
little fallout? You beat me up!'

Ritchie averted his gaze from her bruised face.
'You fell. Don't blame me for it. Let's talk about this
like adults in private.'

'No, thanks. I don't want anything more to do

with you,' Skye countered, backing away and heading for the car.

Ritchie made a sudden lurch in her direction in an effort to cut off her escape, only to be hauled back by Antonio. He twisted free again and swung round to punch the other man but Antonio was too quick on his feet. Moving out of reach, Antonio quickly climbed into the car, which pulled away as soon as he closed the door. Breathless and shaken by Ritchie's continuing aggression, Skye was very relieved that Alana was looking after the children and that Brodie hadn't been subjected to another violent scene. Tears stung her eyes while Antonio and Matteo talked in their own language.

'He's following us,' Antonio informed her.

Skye suppressed a groan. She hadn't wanted Ritchie to find out where she was staying. She resisted the urge to twist round in her seat and look.

'Whatever you want. We're on call. The boss doesn't want us leaving you alone anywhere,' Matteo explained. 'And after what I just witnessed, that's definitely the right decision.'

Her mobile phone buzzed. 'How are you?' Enzo asked huskily.

'A bit shaken up. Very grateful I wasn't on my own,' she confided, thinking that he had the most beautiful voice, dark and deep, edged with his purring accent. 'I'm sorry I'm being such a nuisance.'

'That's not what I think, *piccolo mio*. Just make sure you keep my men with you.'

Enzo finished the call as the firm's head of marketing hovered, a languorous light in her appreciative gaze as the sinuous brunette studied him with naked longing. He had had a difficult first day. Stripping out the top-heavy management layer in the company would gain him no friends. As for the new ideas he had brought with him, they were no more welcome except to the few who'd had the foresight to see a more prosperous future for the firm.

'My girlfriend,' Enzo lied smoothly.

Martina had spent the day trying to flirt with him, brush against him, catch his attention. He wanted her to back off and the pretence that he already had a woman in his life was the easiest cure for what ailed her. Regrettably, Enzo was all too well accustomed to women who threw themselves at him. He was rich, young and single and such pronounced attention went with the territory. Being hunted and propositioned didn't turn him on and he did not want that complication in the workplace.

'I thought you were in England alone, Mr Durante,' Martina remarked.

Enzo cursed the notoriety of his name. Of course, the staff knew who he was: Lorenzo Durante, dubbed the Playboy Prince by the Italian media, a moniker he had inherited from his late father, whose legendary exploits with women had destroyed his marriage soon after Enzo was born. He and his wife had been in the throes of their last attempt at reconciliation when they had died together.

'I'm not.' He murmured the untruth without hesitation and found himself thinking with helpless longing of Skye, who had no notion of flirting with him or jumping his bones. It was a new experience for him to be treated as an adult man, rather than a fabulously rich asset to be acquired. It was also oddly restful.

Alana was an invaluable help when their possessions were loaded willy-nilly into the hall. 'It's truly over with Ritchie?' she prompted hopefully as she set the high chair into the kitchen. 'You know he'll come after you and apologise and maybe even grovel and promise that it won't ever happen again.'

'It doesn't matter. It's over for ever and ever,' Skye confirmed. 'I don't ever want to see him again. He saw us leaving and he was still in a temper.'

Alana frowned. 'Tell me about the businessman who owns this place,' she urged.

Skye made coffee for everyone and allowed Brodie to take his trike out into the back garden with Sparky because it was fully enclosed by a fence.

While helping to feed Shona in her high chair, Skye filled in the details about what had happened the night before.

'And there's nothing icky about this guy Enzo?' Alana pressed suspiciously.

'No, definitely no ick factor there. To be honest, he's gorgeous but I don't have any worries in that direction. I imagine he goes for much more glamorous types than me.'

'I'm worried because I honestly don't think Ritchie is going to leave you alone. He's more likely to act like a stalker, always wanting to know your business,' Alana murmured anxiously. 'I think you need to report him to the police. What if he finds you on your own and attacks you again?'

Skye mulled that thorny question over while Alana helped her get unpacked and persuaded her to choose the bedroom next door to hers for the children, because there was more space and storage. There were *six* bedrooms in total and she could always double up with the children if Enzo was entertaining and needed an extra room. The unpacking achieved, Skye mustered her shopping list and rang Antonio to tell him that she was ready to go into town. Alana offered to accompany her to help her with the kids.

As they left the supermarket laden with shopping, Alana took the children straight to her car and Paola took the trolley from Skye. 'You shouldn't be pushing that,' she told Skye firmly.

As the older woman returned to the car to unload the trolley, Ritchie stepped into view between two cars and grabbed Skye's arm. 'Who are those people you are with?' he demanded angrily. 'Who owns that house you're staying in?'

'Let me go!'

As he leant down to her, she smelt the alcohol on him and grimaced. 'It's over, Ritchie. Let go of my arm.'

'Let go of my sister!' Alana seethed, running up to intervene and aiming a kick at the blond man.

In a fury, Ritchie swung round as Skye finally broke free of him, and found Antonio in his path. But it was Paola who surged forward, seemingly out of nowhere, and took Ritchie down with a martial arts move, dragged his hands behind his back and, with a remarkable lack of drama, handed him over to the security guard approaching them.

'Now you know why you have to go to the police,' Paola said quietly as Skye, white-faced and trembling, accompanied her sister back to her car. 'That man is going to continue coming after you. He's angry and stubborn.'

'I'll do it this evening,' she promised shakily.

Skye started dinner. But before she even got half-way through her preparations, Enzo strode into the kitchen. 'Your sister has agreed to stay with your siblings. I'm here to take you to the police station before you lose your nerve.'

Skye tensed. 'But—'

'You have no choice,' he reminded her.

No, she had had no choices while she was living with Ritchie, Skye conceded, thinking of all the times she had given way to Ritchie to placate him. But now she was supposed to be leading her life again and making her own choices. Even so, it seemed that reclaiming her freedom required more from her than simply walking away from Ritchie: it meant she had to *fight*. Not go apologetically about her business, certainly not depend on Enzo's employees to protect her. She had to fight and stand on her own two feet.

'Okay. Maybe I should get changed first,' she said, smoothing damp palms down her slender thighs, feeling that her jeans and long-sleeved T-shirt might be too casual.

'You'll do fine as you are,' Enzo asserted as she went into the cloakroom to retrieve her padded jacket, wincing as she slid her arms into the sleeves.

He's gorgeous! Alana mouthed at her in wonderment when she glanced into the sitting room where her sister was now sitting with the children. Skye went pink and glanced uneasily at Enzo. He needed a shave. His strong jawline was shadowed by blue-black stubble. He also looked a little weary and her heart smote her without warning. He should have been coming home to relax and eat.

'I was planning such a good meal for dinner,' she confided guiltily.

'It'll keep until later.'

'But you must be hungry,' she protested as he led her outside into the cold crisp air.

'Take the sunshades off,' he urged.

Skye lowered them to blink at him. Her bruised eye was opening again and now he saw the unusual colour of them in the artificial light. A violet blue so light and soft it reminded him of lilac blossom in the spring. His lush black lashes came down low over his eyes and he turned his head away, irritated by that momentary distraction. 'Let's go,' he urged.

Skye climbed awkwardly into the passenger seat. There was no avoiding the step up into the car, no way that every movement of her body could fail to jar her ribs. She grimaced, wondering about that strange moment when Enzo had stared down at her. He had wanted to see how she looked and the news was nothing good. The bruises round her eye had turned all the colours of the rainbow and had only deepened overnight, but at least her eye was opening again.

The instant they arrived at the police station, Enzo requested a senior officer, his quiet confidence patent. Shown into an interview room, Enzo explained why they had asked for a senior officer. A female officer was called and Skye was shown into another interview room, this time without Enzo by her side, where she explained what had happened with Ritchie. After she had made a statement, she had to wait for a police doctor to arrive and undergo an examination and have her injuries photographed. Not once did anyone refer to the fact that her assailant was a policeman who worked under the same roof as them. That professional attitude eased Skye's surging tension.

By the time she saw Enzo again, she was exhausted and her throat was sore from all the talking she'd had to do. He escorted her back out to the car. 'Paola and the rest of her team are witnesses and will go in tomorrow to make statements,' he explained. 'I also think you need to ask for a non-molestation order to be placed on your ex. I've arranged for you to consult a solicitor about that tomorrow.'

'You've had to go to an enormous amount of trouble on my behalf.' Skye groaned in embarrassment. 'Why did you bother?'

'First of all, now that you're working for me, your safety is my responsibility. Second, your ex cannot be allowed to get away with hurting and threatening you, nor can he be permitted to continue working in a position of trust. Thirdly, the children must be assured of a safe environment.'

'You only met me yesterday,' Skye reminded him. 'Don't you wish you had simply driven on past?'

Enzo shrugged a broad shoulder and filtered the car back down the driveway. 'Here we are, home to the haunted house.'

'Why do you call it that?'

'That's what it reminds me of…the era and the décor. If we don't have a ghost, I'll feel short-changed.'

'So, you don't own this place?'

'No, I assume it's rented. My grandfather made the arrangements for my stay. By the way, your sister had to leave to go to work. Paola took over as babysitter.'

There she went again, Skye thought in embarrassment. She was one big problem. Employing her when she came with two children was more hassle than any job she could do would be worth.

'I had no work to do. Your sister put the children to bed before she left,' Paola told her soothingly. 'Do you feel better now that you've reported him?'

'Yes,' Skye fibbed because, in truth, she felt worse and more scared than ever because Ritchie would be enraged that she had gone to the police to report the assault.

As Paola departed, Skye went into the kitchen to start the meal she had planned. Enzo appeared in the doorway. 'You can cook tomorrow night. I've ordered a meal from the hotel your sister works for to be delivered for both of us. It's late and you're exhausted.'

'Cooking is supposed to be my job,' Skye reminded him stubbornly.

'And tonight, you're having a night off.'

She wanted to argue with him but there was a hard edge to his fabulous bone structure that persuaded her to accept his wishes. 'You're tired too,' she conceded. 'What was your first day like?'

'Bloody,' he confided with a feeling grimace.

Skye went into the dining room to set the table for the meal. She put the electric fire on to make it less gloomy and lit the lamp on the corner table. Enzo had gone upstairs and when he reappeared, his hair was still damp from the shower and he was clad in faded jeans that fitted him like a glove and a grey sweater. For a split second she found herself staring and she quickly caught herself and moved past him to fill a jug with cold water and bring glasses.

For goodness' sake, she worked for the guy. Agreed, he was breathtakingly handsome and her heart had skipped a beat as he'd walked into the room, but she had to bury those kinds of female responses and pay no heed to such promptings. Fortunately for her, she was not the most ravishing woman on the planet so he was highly unlikely to look at her in the same way.

'What made it a bloody day?' she asked quietly.

'Redundancies, but if business goes the way I hope we'll be hiring more people in the near future,' he pointed out. 'That's how it goes.'

'Is it Mackies, the packaging factory in the industrial estate that was bought out?' Skye asked. 'Mackies is the main employer around here.'

Enzo nodded as the doorbell chimed.

Skye went to answer the door and stepped back as a heated trolley was trundled in complete with waiter.

'In here…' Enzo instructed. 'Sit down, Skye.'

Awkwardly she took a seat at the table when she had planned to take her plate through to the kitchen.

'We'll serve ourselves,' Enzo decreed.

'I'll do it,' Skye offered, registering that there was an entire three-course meal awaiting them and utterly taken aback by the lavish quality of the food.

The salad starter was set out first and the desserts laid on the sideboard.

'This is lovely,' Skye said warmly. 'I wasn't expecting such a spread.'

She shook out her napkin and began to eat with appetite.

Enzo told her that the company was to begin selling biodegradable packaging, which was currently much in demand. To enable that switch, new machinery would be installed in the factory and there was already a large contract in the pipeline. 'I think my *nonno*…my grandfather tailored this job for my benefit.'

'How?'

'I own one of the largest companies that provide packaging of that kind in the world,' he admitted with the utmost casualness. 'My grandfather hoped that I would have a personal interest in setting up a new business in that field.'

The main course was served while Enzo talked.

Although she had never thought about packaging much, she was a keen recycler. When the waiter departed with the trolley, leaving them to attend to the desserts, she was relieved not to have anyone else listening to their conversation, although she had noticed that that silent third presence had not inhibited Enzo in the slightest. Every minute in his company, she was learning something new about him. Seemingly, Lorenzo Durante was much richer than she had assumed. The largest company...*in the world*? She should have checked him out on the Internet, she thought wryly. Clearly, he was accustomed to having people wait on him.

'Did you have an argument with your ex?' Enzo intoned quietly, once they were alone. 'Is that what started the assault?'

'No, there was no argument. He came home from work in a foul mood,' Skye explained heavily. 'He had found out that he had failed the exam he needs to pass to go for promotion. It was the third time he'd failed and he blamed us for it.'

'How?'

'He blew up in a rage, shouting that it was impossible for him to study with the kids around,' Skye proffered, her soft mouth compressing. 'I made the mistake of trying to reason with him. I didn't remind him that he had failed the exam twice before we moved in or that I only saw him trying to study *once*. I just said that the next time I would take the children out and that's when he went over the edge because, apparently, he can't sit the exam again until next year. He punched me and called me stuff and when I fell, he went for my throat. I honestly thought he was going to kill me…'

Enzo swore in Italian under his breath. 'I'm sorry I brought it up again.'

'It happened.' Skye lifted and dropped a shoulder and then stood up to fetch the desserts from the sideboard. 'But he'd never hit me before. I wouldn't have stayed with him if he had.'

'How long were you with him?'

For an instant, Skye focused on his eyes, amber gold in the low light, enhanced by spiky black lashes, and her mouth ran dry.

'Skye?'

'Oh, you asked me a question,' she recalled belatedly, her face burning with discomfiture because she had zoned out just looking at his eyes. 'We were together four months, not very long really. But it wasn't working for me. He was controlling, possessive, suspicious of every move I made. He didn't want me to have friends, he didn't even like me seeing Alana. It's a challenge to act normally with someone like that and, more and more, I felt like a cat on hot bricks around him. If it hadn't been for the children and my reluctance to disrupt their lives again, I wouldn't have stayed as long as I did with him.'

'Will you go back into teaching?'

'If I can find a job that doesn't entail moving miles away from my sister, yes. Did you get any word about my car?'

'Yes.' Enzo sighed. 'There's so much wrong with it, you'd be wiser letting it go to the scrapyard.'

'No!' Skye cut in, her dismay obvious. 'Mavis was my mum's car and she's irreplaceable.'

Enzo studied her in disbelief. 'Mavis? You actually *named* that hunk of junk?'

'Mum did.' Skye stood up. 'I'll go and fetch the coffee. I got the machine working. I even ground the beans.'

'The car has sentimental value?'

'Yes. Mavis comes with a carload of childhood happy memories.'

'At least you *knew* your mother. Mine died with my father when I was six weeks old,' Enzo admitted. 'A car accident. My grandparents raised me.'

'Photographs aren't much of a comfort, are they?' Skye quipped as she hovered beside him on her way out of the door to the kitchen. Without thought, she squeezed his shoulder in consolation. 'At least you have grandparents. Mine were long gone by the time my mother and stepfather passed away.'

Enzo blinked in shock at that affectionate shoulder squeeze. The only person who had ever touched him like that was his grandmother. Outside the bedroom door, Enzo was unaccustomed to such gestures, and in the bedroom he usually avoided that kind of intimacy because it was likely to give women the wrong message. After almost marrying the wrong woman at university, flings had become much more Enzo's style with the opposite sex. There were no misunderstandings or future expectations that way.

A cup of coffee was slid in front of him.

Skye watched him sip and smile with pleasure and she began to clear away the dishes.

'No, sit down and join me,' Enzo urged. 'I have a proposition to put to you.'

Her brow furrowed, her violet eyes widened and flashed with curiosity and he smiled. 'You look like a kitten when you do that.'

Skye pursed her lips. 'Think panther or tiger, definitely *not* kitten.'

And Enzo burst out laughing at that advice. 'I don't think that's likely to work for me, *piccolo mio*. How do you feel about acting as my fake girlfriend at a party next week?' he extended, the laughter still lending a buoyant afterglow to his lean, darkly attractive features. He had charm in spades, she conceded abstractedly, struggling to concentrate.

CHAPTER THREE

'Fake girlfriend?' Skye repeated uncertainly. 'What's a fake girlfriend?'

'A pretend relationship. No sex involved nor, indeed, anything else you might reasonably object to,' Enzo clarified smoothly. 'I have several women coming on to me at work and there's a staff party next week. I would like a platonic girlfriend on my arm to ensure that nobody thinks I'm available. I'm afraid my reputation as a womaniser goes before me but I have no intention of getting involved with anyone while I'm here.'

Skye wasn't surprised that women were making advances to him. He was exceedingly well built and extraordinarily gorgeous. Any single woman would look twice and hang out a welcome sign, but she was shocked that he could so lightly refer to having a reputation as a womaniser. 'A womaniser?' she queried with a wrinkled nose of distaste.

'Believe it or not, that attracts some women. Right

now, however, I'm living the celibate life,' Enzo quipped with a wry curve of his lips. 'And I intend to continue to do so while I'm here.'

'Good to know,' Skye countered, feeling her cheeks burn. 'So, you want a fake girlfriend to keep you safe from temptation.'

'*Sì*... No affairs, no one-nighters and no entanglements of any kind,' he spelt out.

'But nobody would credit me in a role like that. I'm not stylish enough for someone like you,' she said ruefully.

'Your bruises will have faded by the end of next week and clever make-up will take care of any marks that linger. I will naturally cover the expense of an outfit for the occasion as I doubt you have anything suitable.'

'I'll think about it. I suppose I could do it as a favour in return for all that you've done for me,' Skye conceded quietly.

'I'm not a fan of favours. I'll *pay* you for doing it.'

'No. The party will be my thank you for you helping us last night and for coming to the police station with me this evening,' Skye countered with quiet dignity. 'I'm not a hired escort. I'll do it for free, so please don't offer me money again.'

Enzo's dark as night eyes positively shimmered. 'Is that a warning?'

'Yes,' Skye confirmed, rising to start clearing the

table. 'Will you be wanting anything else tonight? I was thinking of having an early night.'

'Go to bed. I'll see you in the morning.'

Skye paused at the door and then turned back, unable to resist saying, 'Isn't it crazy that we've only known each other for twenty-four hours?'

Enzo thought about that and he was equally taken aback by the reminder. It was rare for him to feel so comfortable with a woman and yet, in reality, he barely knew Skye. Perhaps that was because he knew nothing could happen between them, he reasoned thoughtfully. Perhaps he relaxed more with her as a result of that awareness. And possibly she was comfortable with him for the exact same reason. In any case it would take her a while to get over the abusive creep she had been living with. In addition, posing as his fake girlfriend might give her an extra layer of protection against her ex, he reflected wryly.

His grandmother called him to catch up and he told her at length about finding Skye and her siblings and the dog by the side of the road.

'You're not getting involved with this young woman?' she questioned worriedly. 'I'm proud that you helped her, but I wouldn't want you hurting her by taking too much of an interest in her.'

'No, there's nothing of that nature between us. She's totally safe with me. The kids are quite cute, though,' he remarked, something of his surprise at that discovery clear in his voice.

* * *

A womaniser? Skye lay in bed and played with her phone, slotting his name into a search engine and then reading results. It took a couple of attempts to spell his name correctly and then a cascade of results tumbled onto the screen. She saw a photo of him half naked in shorts on a yacht with a gaggle of blonde tanned beauties surrounding him. Suddenly feeling like a disrespectful snoop, she closed the site and put her phone down. Enzo's personal life was none of her business and he was entitled to his privacy.

Skye rose early and had the children fed and dressed before Enzo even got downstairs. There was no reason to subject him to the early morning chaos of life with young children, she reasoned. 'I planned to serve your breakfast in the dining room,' she remarked when he strode into the kitchen.

As usual, at first glimpse, Enzo knocked the breath right out of her lungs. Sheathed in a light grey, exquisitely tailored suit that lovingly outlined his broad shoulders, lean hips and long powerful legs, he looked amazing. Everything he wore fitted him to perfection. She wondered how many suits he owned because she had yet to see him in the same one twice.

'I'm happy enough to eat in here… *Dio mio!*' he exclaimed in apparent astonishment as Shona crawled across the floor towards him. 'She moves on her own!'

Helplessly amused by his fascination, Skye watched her sister claw her way upright by dint of clutching Enzo's legs. 'I'll put her out in the hall,' she said abruptly.

'No need. She's not doing any harm,' Enzo declared as Brodie, hungry for his attention, brought him a toy car to examine. 'What age are they?'

'Brodie is almost three and Shona's thirteen months.' Skye ferried coffee to him and plucked Shona from his knees to give him some peace. She remained convinced that he should be sitting in the dining room where she had laid the table for him. She would never forget his conviction that the microwave would make his toast for him. She suspected that Enzo was woefully unacquainted with kitchens and with eating his meals against such a humble backdrop. Furthermore, he was only making do with her as a housekeeper because she had already been on his doorstep and an easily available option.

Enzo ate only part of the supermarket croissant, his aristocratic nose wrinkling a tad, and she resolved to try the bakery in town for a substitute. Instinct warned her that Enzo was accustomed to only the very best. He didn't like the house and was certainly not impressed by it, yet it was large and warm and had been sensitively renovated with modern utilities while retaining all the features that gave it character. There were probably many things in life that Enzo Durante took entirely for granted, she decided ruefully.

'You are looking very serious,' Enzo commented.

'I was just thinking that you don't really appreciate this house,' she heard herself admit. 'And yet it's very comfortable and in excellent order.'

'You sound like my conscience speaking,' Enzo retaliated with a groan as he sliced an apple into slim segments. 'I agree that it's functional, but I prefer a contemporary style. My grandparents live in an old ancestral house and that is probably why he chose this place for me.'

'You're spoiled,' Skye responded before she could bite back the words.

A slanting grin slashed Enzo's lean, hard-boned face, unhidden amusement glittering in his very dark eyes. 'Probably,' he agreed equably.

'I'm sorry. I shouldn't have said that.' Skye's cheeks were wreathed in pink and embarrassment engulfed her. Who was she to criticise him? His laid-back manner had momentarily betrayed her into forgetting that he was her employer.

'I don't take offence easily,' Enzo riposted, enjoying the way the blush made her eyes look lighter in hue and enthralled by the habit she had of looking down, her feathery lashes drooping when she was embarrassed while her teeth plucked at the edge of her full lower lip. 'I have many choices others don't enjoy and I should be more aware of that. I also like an honest woman, who isn't out to impress me and watching her every word.'

'But I should be watching every word,' Skye replied. 'I *should* be behaving professionally.'

'But your profession isn't housekeeping and we're alone in this house, so obviously we can't ignore each other,' Enzo pronounced with an air of finality as he vaulted upright. 'I'll text you with the time of your appointment with the solicitor.'

'I can take care of that for myself.'

'It's halfway to being organised already,' Enzo told her as he turned away.

'Thanks, then,' Skye said awkwardly, grabbing Brodie as he tried to follow Enzo out into the hall.

The interview with the solicitor later that morning was a sobering experience because it brought up everything she had crammed down to the very bottom of her memory. She didn't want to remember what Ritchie had done to her because the recollection of how she had lain on the floor pretending to be unconscious to avoid further injury still made her cringe. It wasn't an image she wanted to have of herself and she knew that she would never again put herself in such a position with the children.

Her thoughts, however, were slowly becoming less negative and self-critical. It wasn't her fault that Ritchie had turned out to be violent and nasty. There had been no warning of his explosion of rage and subsequent attack. But possibly, if she hadn't feared moving the children and disrupting their lives all over again, she would have told him sooner that the relationship wasn't working for her.

That evening, Enzo found himself dining in the solitary splendour of the dining room and he felt ridiculously lonely. Skye had informed him that she had already eaten and she was bathing the kids upstairs. From somewhere above, he could hear the sound of Brodie's giggles. Boundaries, he thought. Skye was carefully marking boundaries, reminding him that she worked for him and making it clear that she would stick to the rules…even though he hadn't laid down *any* rules.

In defiance, he climbed the stairs and followed the noise. Brodie was capering around the main bathroom half dressed in dinosaur pyjama bottoms while Skye endeavoured to insert a squirming Shona into what he believed was known as a onesie. Flushed and very damp, her tee clinging to her slight curves, Skye looked harassed and as Brodie charged at him in welcome, Enzo picked up the discarded pyjama top and corralled Brodie to put it on him. The little boy startled him by winding his arms round his neck and forcing Enzo to lift him.

'Thanks. Sorry we were so noisy,' Skye muttered. 'They both sort of wind up at bedtime.'

'They're in the room next door to you?' Enzo

checked. 'I'll put him in there. How did the meeting go with the solicitor?'

'He was very efficient and the police phoned me. Ritchie has been suspended from duty pending investigation.'

Enzo lowered Brodie to the bed and watched him snatch up a scruffy rabbit soft toy, pressing it to his chest and turning over, all liveliness draining away as evidently the day's activities caught up with him. Shaking loose the duvet to cover him, Enzo straightened as Skye settled her sister into the cot.

'The solicitor thinks there's sufficient evidence for Ritchie to be arrested and charged,' she told him quietly, something of her mental turmoil showing in her troubled gaze. 'I can't get past the fact that I thought he loved me and yet he did *that* to me.'

Enzo lounged in the doorway, his big frame lithe and sleek and relaxed as she switched out the light. 'I thought a woman loved me once but it went badly wrong, although she didn't assault me,' he remarked with graveyard humour, brooding dark eyes glinting beneath lush black lashes. 'Now I steer clear of the love thing...'

His blunt candour disconcerted her and as he stepped back to allow her to partially close the door of the children's room, she winced and sighed. 'As will I in the future.'

CHAPTER FOUR

'IT'S LIKE BEING a princess for the day!' Alana carolled. 'I'm so envious I'm ashamed of myself!'

'Alana...' Skye felt guilty and rather vain for being equally thrilled by her elegant, groomed appearance in the mirror.

It was so very long since she had seen herself polished up to her best. The last time had been for a formal dance at college in her final year. A visit to the beauty salon at the exclusive hotel where her sister worked had transformed her hair and the professional but subtle make-up covered her fading bruises to perfection. Her rebellious curls had been tamed into glossy honey-blonde ringlets that tumbled artfully down to her slim shoulders. The dress, in the palest shade of lilac, was fashioned in a glistening fabric that caught the light and came to mid-thigh, short enough to be fashionable, long enough not to be daring. Her arms were bare, and an unusual toning collar of artificial pearls contrived to conceal the marks on her neck. The stylist, whom Enzo had organised to come to the house, had brought a selection of cocktail dresses for her to choose from. She slid her feet into the delicate high heels and lifted the beaded purse and shawl that completed the outfit.

'Well, when did either of us last have any fun?' Her sister sighed. 'We lost Mum and Dad and it was one long struggle to survive afterwards. There was no time and no money for girly stuff and remembering that we were still young.'

And that was true, horribly true, Skye conceded with regret. In the midst of their shock and grief, she and Alana had made the decision to step into their late parents' shoes for Brodie and Shona's sake and that had entailed serious sacrifices. Initially, it had been a long, dreary haul, working hard to meet the bills, find employment and somewhere affordable to live. Alana had insisted on dropping out of university, as determined as Skye to do the very best she could for their younger siblings.

Skye turned back to her sister. 'I promise that you and I will have a night out some time soon and relive exactly what it is like to *be* young.'

Alana's eyes lit up and then fell again. 'We'll need a babysitter.'

'We'll find one,' Skye declared and hugged the younger woman. 'We'll look for somewhere where we can live together after Christmas, when Enzo leaves.'

'I *have* to live in at the hotel,' Alana reminded her

with a frown. 'Even if I get this assistant night-shift manager promotion, I'll still have to live in.'

'We'll cope, but maybe get to spend more time together, make it more about us than about the kids,' Skye proposed. 'The little ones do get star billing all the time!'

'But that's what makes you a great second mum,' the blonde told her a little chokily, her eyes filming with tears.

Skye was a little misty-eyed and touched by her sister's faith in her. Enzo strode out of the sitting room. Over the past ten days, she had seen surprisingly little of him and her attention locked onto him as though he were a magnet and she an iron filing. He was working long hours, leaving very early in the morning and rarely coming back before nine in the evening. Sparky was on his heels as usual. Sparky, their late parents' pet, had always preferred men and had once been her stepfather's shadow. Now Sparky was like a horse out of the starting gate the instant he heard Enzo's car pulling up.

He wore yet another different suit, but this one had a designer hip edge of fashion that could have come straight off a Paris catwalk, and the man within that beautiful light grey suit teamed with a dark roll neck was as sleekly, smoothly and smoulderingly sexy as a movie star. That very thought shook her. She didn't look at men and think...hmm, he's sexy, but Enzo was in a class all of his own and very good at knocking her off balance. Not a thought she should be having about him, absolutely not, she censured herself and wiped her mind blank of all such embarrassing stuff.

Enzo stared intently as Skye approached him. 'You look amazing,' he murmured sincerely, rather taken aback by just how beautiful she looked, his gleaming dark gaze flaming to gold and his appraisal lingering. There was a lightness in her shy smile and a glow in her face. As he had hoped, she had enjoyed a day of pampering, a day unshaded by the turmoil her ex-boyfriend had plunged her into.

Her curls framed her heart-shaped face, brushing against her fine flushed cheekbones, and the make-up had been applied brilliantly to cover the dark shadowing that still marred her eye. The colour of that dress, that particular shade of lavender, lit up her eyes like stars. The bespoke fit enhanced her diminutive frame, only hinting at her slender curves while putting a pair of award-winning legs and dainty ankles on display. The hardening at his groin was as familiar as it was forbidden, and Enzo breathed in slow and deep to steady himself. She trusted him and he would not betray that trust.

He was well aware that he was attracted to her and that he shouldn't be. He grasped her hand in his. 'You're cold.' He swept the light shawl from her loose hold, shook it out and draped it deftly round her.

'Thanks,' Skye murmured, suddenly unsure of

him and the weirdly tense intimacy of the moment. She lowered her eyes to avoid his clear dark golden gaze. He was so polite, so protective and concerned for her comfort. She wasn't used to those qualities in a man. Ritchie had been hewn from a much rougher rock and she had told herself that that was his tough upbringing, not any lack in him. She supposed that that had been her making excuses for him, overlooking his flaws, refusing to see the bigger picture and that she had picked a man who had *no* caring, respectful side to his character.

As she parted from her sister, Alana bent her head and whispered, 'Enzo is so *hot* for you.'

'No way!' Skye laughed, lest Enzo guess that her sister had been talking about him because Alana had never been a good dissembler and Enzo was as observant as he was quick on the uptake. He was also, she had discovered that very day, chaotically untidy.

'Why didn't you tell me that you were still living out of suitcases and garment bags?' she asked in reproach as she joined him in his car. 'I only found out when I went into your room to change the bed this morning.'

'*Sì*...you've got me all sorted out now. I intended to thank you. At least I can see the floor now,' he remarked with amusement.

Skye gritted her teeth on a tart response. 'Are you aware that all your shirts are dry-clean only?' she continued.

'On the domestic front I am…pretty useless,' Enzo conceded after a moment's pause. 'But I shine in other fields.'

'I put the shirts into the dry-cleaners in town. Which other fields?'

'I'm good at dealing with people…as long as I'm sober,' he qualified, thinking back darkly a couple of months to the dinner party that he had unwisely attended at his grandparents' home. 'I'm innovative in business and courteous. I was very well raised. I've also discovered to my surprise that I can work very hard when I'm challenged and that my concentration is stellar.'

'You're used to maids picking up after you though, aren't you?'

'I would prefer not to answer that question on the grounds that I suspect that some kind of moral judgement is likely to come my way,' Enzo replied.

'Any other fields in which you shine?' she prompted, ready to change the subject because it wasn't her place to nag when he was paying her to take care of everything on the domestic front.

'I speak several languages fluently. I'm good at negotiation. I'm supposed to be terrific in bed but then women will always tell you that, if you're rich,' he quipped wryly, shocking her with his candour. 'Am I allowed to ask if you shine there as well?'

Skye had grown very tense. She knew that he had recognised that she was nervous of the evening ahead and that he was trying to distract her to get her to relax. It was just unfortunate that he had stumbled on that particular subject. 'I don't…shine, I mean,' she told him tightly. 'In fact, I have it on recent authority that I'm rubbish in that line. And I really don't care if it's true or not. I don't like sex. It does nothing for me.'

Having stopped at the traffic lights, Enzo flicked her a frowning glance. 'He *was* a charmer, wasn't he? He was putting you down. He seems to have been the sort of guy who likes to keep a woman down. Don't pay any heed to his opinion.'

'I'm not. I was just being frank, possibly *too* frank,' she muttered uneasily, her cheeks belatedly burning like fire in the dimness of the car. 'Shouldn't we be talking about this evening? Who am I supposed to be?'

'Yourself, of course. My girlfriend. Teacher, currently too busy with me and your siblings to work.'

'Girlfriend?'

'You're living with me. I have no intention of telling anyone that you're my housekeeper.'

'Ashamed?'

'*Dio mio*…it's simpler for us both if we pretend to be together this evening,' Enzo responded. 'I could have called half a dozen women in London to come up here and act the part but there would've been strings and expectations attached, and I didn't want that complication. You're doing me a huge favour and I appreciate it.'

'It's costing you enough…the trip to the Blackthorn Hotel beauty spa and the outfit I'm wearing did not, I suppose, come cheap,' Skye reminded him. 'And really…? *Half a dozen* women would have been willing to drop everything and come up here on short notice just to please you?'

'It's the wealth I inherited that's the draw, not me as an individual,' he breathed with sardonic bite.

'Maybe for some of them but I doubt it's the driving motivation for *all* of them,' Skye told him mildly. 'I mean, stop being such a cynic. Some of those ladies may just like you.'

'Do you?' he asked her unexpectedly.

Skye shot him an unexpectedly sunny smile. 'Yes, I do. You have a great deal of charm, which I'm sure you're well aware of, and you've been kind to the kids. If you're kind to my siblings, I become a big fan. Oh…random question here. Why were all the frocks the stylist brought some shade of purple? Is it your favourite colour?'

Enzo laughed. 'No, your eyes are the colour of lilacs, and I thought a similar shade would suit you.'

Skye shot him an unimpressed glance. 'They're not lilac. My goodness, I only wish they were! Lilac sounds exotic. Actually, they're a greyish light blue,' she told him informatively.

'Lilac,' Enzo repeated stubbornly as he turned

down the road to the Blackthorn Hotel where her sister worked and the Mackies executive dinner was being held.

'Oh, my goodness, so where are we supposed to have met?'

'Your car broke down. Always best to stick as close to the truth as possible. Of course, the car breakdown happened months ago,' Enzo mocked. 'I'm not the sort of crazy guy who would invite a woman I've only known a few hours to live with me.'

'Aren't you?' Skye sent him a winging look of amusement. 'It's my bet that you can be impulsive and that you pride yourself on your ability to judge character.'

Enzo shot her an arrested glance, for that surmise had struck a little too close to home for comfort. 'Do you think you could act keen and clingy at this event for my benefit?'

Skye heaved a long-suffering sigh. 'If I worked at it. I'm not the clingy type and I imagine that you hate clingers.'

'I do,' Enzo confirmed, closing an arm round her for show and walking her towards the hotel entrance. 'But I'm fed up with the ambitious sex bombs at Mackies coming on to me and a clingy girlfriend will tell them that they're wasting their time.'

'I won't let you out of my sight,' Skye promised with amusement.

As drinks were served in an anteroom, Skye was

conscious of being the cynosure of curious eyes. Enzo introduced her to the executives, including three very attractive brunettes, garbed in dresses that were very short and harboured strategic cut-outs that played up their ample bosoms and curvy behinds.

'You're sisters,' she guessed, having registered that they all had the same surname. 'And the daughters of the Mackie family, who originally owned the firm?'

'Your boyfriend hasn't made the same connection,' Martina, the head of marketing, informed her rather smugly.

'I would doubt that,' Skye countered gently, well aware that she enjoyed access through Enzo to confidential information and she knew that he believed that the firm had been ruined by placing highly paid family members in executive positions, even though they had few qualifications and little experience. 'He doesn't miss much.'

'You're a little petite to be a model,' Martina remarked. 'I was so sure you would be a model. Lorenzo has a long track record of dating models.'

Skye didn't bat an eyelash at that tactless reference to Enzo's past. She simply smiled and mentioned that she was a teacher, not currently employed.

'What do you think attracted him to you?' one of the sisters asked her with deadly seriousness.

'Skye's a fabulous cook,' Enzo drawled from behind her, tugging her back against him with easy intimacy. 'And the only woman I know who would dare to serve a pasta dish to a native-born Italian!'

'You *liked* it!' Skye reminded him, content to act the couple for the benefit of their audience. 'Most men like mac and cheese. It's a comfort food.'

'But it's not Italian,' Enzo told her, dark eyes glinting, determined to have the last word.

'I don't know how to cook in the Italian style,' Skye admitted calmly as he led her off to join another group.

'Were the Mackie daughters pleasant?'

'Martina was very surprised that I wasn't a model. Apparently, you have an impressive record of dating models,' Skye teased.

'The past is the past and we're leaving it there,' Enzo murmured sibilantly. 'But I haven't *dated* anyone since university.'

'So, you really don't do serious? Is that because you got burned?'

'I like to think I'm a little more mature than that.' Enzo's strong profile tautened. 'Maybe I'm just not ready to settle down yet.'

'Or maybe you missed your *one* by treating her like all her predecessors, like she was just a hook-up and nothing special,' Skye suggested with a wry smile.

Enzo swung back to her as though she had jabbed him with a knife, dark eyes glittering as though he were under attack. 'We have the most extraordinary conversations. Have you noticed that?'

'Not really,' Skye fibbed, not wanting him to appreciate that the way she relaxed with him was exceptional for her in male company, particularly after her ordeal with Ritchie, with whom an unguarded word could induce a surly silent mood that could last for hours. Yet on instinct she trusted Enzo, she registered in surprise. He wasn't given to moods and she suspected that even if she annoyed him, he would be blunt and straightforward about setting her straight.

'You're insidious.' Enzo gazed down at her with hooded dark eyes that glinted in the low light. 'You make sneaky little comments that stay with me.'

Her lilac eyes gleamed, and she bobbed a mock curtsy as if she were a maid being rebuked by the master of the house while her generous mouth curled into a mischievous grin. 'I'm sorry, sir. I'll try to mind my words better.'

'Like I believe that!' Enzo mocked back, his smile matching her own as he closed an arm round her to guide her into the private dining room.

'What's your secret?' the woman next to her whispered over the soup.

'Excuse me? Sorry, I didn't quite catch what you—'

'You have a notorious international playboy hanging on your every word like a puppy,' the blonde whispered. 'What's your secret? There are women at this table who would kill you and walk over your body to find out.'

Skye flushed. 'Enzo and I are...well, first and foremost, friends,' she selected awkwardly but with quiet sincerity. Friends without benefits, that was what they were, she reasoned, and Enzo was not in any way like a puppy. Puppies were innocent and there was nothing innocent about Enzo. If he seemed to be hanging onto her every word, it was just part of the whole pretence that she was his girlfriend.

'Keep it up. You're breaking the hearts of Macbeth's witches!' The other woman laughed and Skye glanced up to encounter the grim spiteful looks coming her way from the brunette bombshell trio Enzo had warned her about.

'The Witches. That's what they're called at work. I believe you're a teacher...'

With relief, Skye relaxed into an uncontroversial topic and another young mother began to talk to her about childhood development. Before she knew where she was, Enzo was tugging her up out of her seat with a rueful look. 'Time to go home,' he chided. 'We promised Alana we wouldn't be late.'

As it wasn't anywhere near late, Skye could only assume that Enzo had had enough of glad-handing and polite conversation. 'Well, you went down well with everyone,' he commented with satisfaction as he tucked her into the car.

'Apparently they call the Mackie daughters Macbeth's witches at work…'

Enzo laughed out loud as he drove off. 'Yes, one can imagine them toiling over a cauldron plotting and making spells.'

'If you turn left just down there, it's a shortcut back into town,' Skye informed him, indicating the country road.

'I haven't been along here before,' Enzo admitted as buildings appeared, marking the outskirts of the town.

'I know it well. I grew up around here,' Skye confided, peering out of the windows and smiling at the familiarity of the street. 'Oh, Enzo, if you're not in a hurry, turn down there. There used to be an ice-cream shop I was last in as a teenager. I bet it's long gone.' She sighed apologetically.

But the ice-cream shop had turned into a small café and Skye beamed. 'I wonder if they still do home-made ice cream.'

'I have the feeling we're about to find out.'

'Do you like ice cream?' she asked him on the pavement, enthusiasm already moving her ahead of him.

He watched her break into an animated chat with the woman behind the counter, who turned out to be the daughter of the original owners. She tasted three different flavours and picked the fudge one, groaning out loud as she savoured it. 'That is *so* good!' she carolled.

Enzo picked vanilla with a lot less animation.

'You're not very adventurous,' she scolded as they got back in the car. 'Gosh, that place brings back so many memories of my parents. It was our local shop back then and on Saturdays, we got ice cream.'

'You must have been a very easily pleased teenager.'

'I'm talking about when I was younger, like still a kid.'

'Are you? You're what…twenty-two or twenty-three? And you seem equally enthusiastic now.' Tawny eyes rested on her with gentle mockery. 'I've given women diamonds and received less appreciation. Give you an ice-cream cone *and…*?'

Skye giggled. 'No, you'd have to give me more than an ice-cream cone,' she warned him, digging into her cone with gusto, little pink tongue swirling round the sweet confection, soft pink lips savouring.

'You've got it on your face now,' Enzo complained, digging a tissue out to wipe the tip of her gently tilted nose clean, the pulse at his groin downright painful. 'Take your time.'

'You've got to eat it quickly or it melts all over your hands.' As she licked her pink lips clean she encountered Enzo's scorching golden gaze. *'What?'* she prompted.

'Throw out the cone and lick me instead,' Enzo stunned her by suggesting.

'Enzo!' she exclaimed in stark reproof.

Then she stilled as she collided with smouldering dark golden eyes. Her heart jumped inside her chest, her mouth running dry as a bone. Little tingles of awareness unlike anything she had ever felt travelled through her slender and now very tense frame.

'Your ice cream is melting,' Enzo warned her as she sat there frozen and staring back at him with wide lilac eyes. 'I didn't intend to bring you to an emergency stop. If you mess up the upholstery, I'll throw a fit!'

'You took me by surprise…you shocked me,' she muttered unevenly, struggling to catch her breath, thoroughly unnerved by the sensations that had shimmied up through her taut body and then down again to a place that had ignited with a burst of warmth that mortified her to the very bone.

Enzo released his breath on a measured hiss. 'Relax. For a moment, I was tempted. But nothing is going to happen unless you want it to. I'm attracted to you. I know I shouldn't be but I'm not perfect, in fact it seems I'm all too human. But you are completely safe with me, *piccolo mio.*'

'Maybe I don't need to be safe…with you,' Skye muttered uncertainly. 'You make me feel things I didn't expect to feel. You make me curious. I know, like you said, I shouldn't be in these circumstances. But the truth is, I am and I'm attracted too.'

Literally trembling from her own daring in being that candid, Skye swallowed convulsively and dropped her head, ashamed of the sheer power of his draw for her. She had barely escaped alive from her last entanglement and wouldn't dream of embarking on another. *But...* There was definitely a *huge* 'but' enmeshed in all her thoughts about Enzo, as if he belonged in a category all of his own. Would one kiss hurt? Men and women kissed all the time. It would hardly be a major event.

'So...' Enzo breathed a touch raggedly, his breathing audible. 'What do you want to do about this?'

'We...we could try a kiss...just *one*,' she stressed, evidently fearful that more than one kiss might push him past all restraint. 'Just to satisfy our curiosity, and we'll probably find out it's not worth our while.'

'Not worth our while,' Enzo repeated thickly, afraid that if he didn't speak, he would laugh out loud at her naivety. One kiss. *One kiss.* Even as a teenager, girls had offered him a great deal more than that. And one kiss wasn't going to do anything to tackle his raging arousal, was it? But then, he reminded himself, it wasn't about what he wanted, it was about what *she* wanted and all she could apparently envisage was a very brief, controlled experiment. It was ridiculous. He knew it was. And yet...

and yet, he was as fascinated and as aroused as if she'd ripped off her clothes and propositioned him.

'Agreed. One kiss,' he asserted not quite levelly. 'It won't give me any expectations either, in case you're worried about that possibility. I won't be demanding anything more. But we'll experiment somewhere else, somewhere we're not in full view of my security team.'

'Why do you have so much security?' Skye asked, relaxing a little again now that touching was no longer imminent. Yet it was an effort to speak, to even think rationally because Enzo tied her up in knots to the extent that she barely recognised herself in his company. She said things to Enzo she had never dreamt of saying to any man. He blew through her defensive barriers as though they didn't exist.

'My father was kidnapped when he was younger than I am now. The kidnappers demanded a ransom. My father's father refused to pay and he was tortured...for weeks,' he completed flatly. 'Ultimately, he was rescued but the experience broke something in him and he was never the same afterwards.'

'Oh, my word,' she whispered sickly.

'That's the only reason I have protection. I have to accept that with my wealth I will always be a target. I have my grandparents equally well protected,' he admitted steadily. 'Security being around all the time, however, is occasionally a pain.'

'But necessary. I get it.' She nodded, shaken by what he had revealed.

'Well, that took me out of the moment,' he confided in a roughened undertone, switching on the engine. 'I'll take you back home now.'

'No...*wait*!' Skye exclaimed, grabbing him by his jacket and practically lurching across the car to cover his mouth with her own. She was driven by something she didn't understand but it was still something stronger than she was, something capable of suppressing her essential lack of confidence in that field. The need to connect with Enzo at that instant was more powerful than almost any urge she had ever experienced, indeed almost on a par with her desperate need to escape Ritchie that awful night when he had attacked her. And now here she was attacking Enzo instead, she reflected in disbelief.

'No, not like that.' Predictably, Enzo took charge, ramming back his seat to the furthest to gain more space, lifting her right down on top of him so that her clumsy, uncomfortable stretching lean towards him was no longer necessary. 'Relax, take your time,' he urged.

'But we're in full view of your security team,' she reminded him, face red as fire.

'I don't care. A kiss is no big deal.'

He brushed his lips gently across hers and she stopped breathing, her heart a racing thud in her eardrums. 'No big deal,' he repeated, lifting his handsome dark head again to look down at her where she trembled on his lap. 'There's no need to be scared—'

'I'm *not* scared!' Skye snapped, hands closing into the lapels of his jacket to yank him back to her with an aggression she had never ever felt before. 'If it's one kiss, you do it properly!'

'Is that so?' Enzo regrouped because he had never been forcibly grabbed before and he finally appreciated that she wasn't in the least afraid of him. 'What would madam find acceptable?'

'Oh, stop it!' she scolded him feverishly, stretching up as she had to do even on his lap to find his wickedly attractive mouth for herself. Her palms framed his hard cheekbones and smoothed down to his stubbled jawline, her fingers enjoying the roughness of that dark shadow. In fact, Enzo gave her a feast of different sensations to revel in. There was the wildly enticing smell of him that close, a sort of spicy, musky cologne-tinged masculinity that called to every sense. There were the fingers gently smoothing over her back and the sheer burning, sizzling excitement of his firm lips moving on hers.

It would have been fair to say that a single kiss had never lit a fire in Enzo before but the slight weight of Skye on top of him when he was already hard enough to pound nails was more than sufficient, especially when added to the little throaty sounds she emitted while she squirmed and pressed closer. In fact, a bushfire could not have been hotter. His tongue delved deep and she shuddered, hands on his shoulders now, her fingers digging into him making him think of other things he could be doing to feed that much-to-be-encouraged enthusiasm. Enzo was on a total high.

A trio of teenage boys stopped on the pavement to catcall and make obscene gestures. The sound of their voices broke the spell. Skye tore her swollen lips from his, as shocked as a nun waking up to an orgy, and removed herself so fast from his lap that she was in danger of whiplash. 'What on earth were we thinking of?' she exclaimed sharply.

Enzo forced a laugh when he didn't feel like laughing. He felt more like getting uncharacteristically violent with the teenagers who had wrecked the most erotic encounter he had had in years. That *had* to be his imagination, he told himself straight away. 'We weren't thinking,' he pointed out drily.

'I can't believe I did that!' Skye erupted in sheer embarrassment.

'It's not like we were having sex,' Enzo shot back at her, pulling the car away from the kerb. 'It was just a stupid kiss. Don't overreact!'

Skye's mortification still threatened to swallow her alive. She had told him that she didn't like sex and then snatched at him like an oversexed maneater! Just a *stupid* kiss. Well, she supposed it was stupid on playboy terms. He probably hadn't done anything that innocent in the last ten years or been greeted with any greater female fervour!

'So what went wrong?' Alana asked Skye as she passed her a cup of tea.

'Why do you think there's anything wrong?' Skye asked, struggling to seem cool and unconcerned.

'*He* came in the door like a tornado and went straight upstairs. You came in all pink and stiff. Obviously, something happened,' her wily sibling pointed out and then frowned anxiously. 'Did he make a pass at you?'

'No, I made a pass at him,' Skye corrected. 'But I don't want to talk about it.'

Alana startled her by grinning and then mock-zipping her mouth before grasping her tea and telling her about Brodie's high jinks at bedtime.

The next morning, Skye decided that Enzo lacked the sensitive gene. She set his breakfast at the dining-room table and he carried it through into the kitchen to sit down opposite her when she was feeling as though if she saw him before the end of the century, it would be too soon.

'Do you always make a major event out of little molehills?' Enzo enquired lazily.

'Don't be smart—'

'One of us has to be.'

Skye's cheeks flamed and she dealt him a speaking look.

It was those lilac eyes, Enzo thought in frustration, they got to him in some weird annoying way and made him feel guilty even when she was thoroughly exasperating him.

'I suppose this is not the optimum time to tell you that Mavis is being delivered back to you today.'

'Seriously?' she gasped in disconcertion.

'Roadworthy this time,' Enzo added a tad smugly. 'Your car was in a dangerous condition.'

'Mum was a care assistant. She didn't earn enough to keep Mavis maintained. Keeping her *on* the road was a big enough challenge.'

'I want another favour from you,' Enzo said bluntly. 'But I know you're not in the mood to hear it, right now.'

CHAPTER FIVE

'I'M NOT A moody person!' Skye proclaimed defensively.

'Either that or you're a little puritanical,' Enzo retorted. 'We shared a single kiss, nothing more.'

'I'm sorry,' Skye framed shakily, reaching for her morning coffee only to meet Enzo's hand instead. Long brown fingers enclosed hers in silence.

Regrettably that silence thrummed like a drumbeat inside her and she dropped her eyes to the table top as her insides liquefied at even that minor physical contact. She felt as if she were burning up and the ache between her legs appalled her. It was exactly that same feeling that had made her want to throw herself at him the night before. No guy had ever made her feel like that, certainly not her ex. It was as terrifying as it was thrilling and it was her problem, *not* his.

'What's the favour?'

'It's a big one this time but, as I own the Blackthorn Hotel, you *could* accommodate me, if you chose to do so, because I can free up your sister to take care of the kids while we're away.'

'You *own* the Blackthorn Hotel?' Skye studied him, eyes wide. 'I thought your family business was related to packaging?'

'Companies diversify.' Enzo shrugged. 'I own hotel chains, property, all sorts of stuff in different fields. The Blackthorn belongs to one of the luxury chains.'

'Oh…' Skye said, shattered by the thought of any one man owning so many businesses because it made the extent of his wealth much more obvious and real to her. And you don't like that, do you? She scolded herself with a mentally curled lip of scorn. After all, the richer Enzo was, the more out of her league he was. As if he weren't already out of her league! With his devastating good looks and charisma and even hotter kisses, never mind the playboy reputation that would enhance him in the eyes of some women.

'This favour?'

Enzo let go of her fingers to make an uncharacteristically jerky gesture and frowned. 'I refuse to go into any details but, two months ago, I went to a dinner party drunk with a drunk and not very ladylike partner and something very embarrassing happened. I was in disgrace with my family. *Madre di Dio*… I made my grandmother *cry*…'

'Everyone makes mistakes, Enzo.' Skye recaptured his hand to smooth the back of it gently, recognising that the recollection still filled him with regret.

'You're very tactile…' Enzo breathed.

Skye reddened and immediately let go of his hand, clasping her hands together on her lap to keep them from temptation. 'It's the kids. I'm always touching them, and it gets to be a habit. Sorry.'

Enzo didn't know how to tell her that he liked her easy way of touching him because if he did admit that he would be giving her the wrong impression, wouldn't he? Creating complications he didn't need, possibly hurting her as well, not a risk he should take, he acknowledged grimly.

'Look, I have to go up to Glasgow to see this old guy who is a silent partner in Mackies with my grandfather. He's entitled to a personal report on the firm. But Robinson Davies was at that ghastly dinner party in Italy with his wife and everyone present was very shocked by what happened. I could do with some company to get through lunch with the couple.'

'What happened?'

'I already said that I'm not going to give you the details. Not even thumbscrews would get that confession out of me,' he stated with a sardonic twist of his beautiful stubborn mouth. 'But will you accompany me to Glasgow if your sister is able to stay here to take care of the kids?'

Skye thought about it in the space of a moment.

She knew she should say no. She knew that further extended exposure to Lorenzo Durante was bad for her and that she would be wiser to avoid him to the best of her ability. But she also knew how much she owed him for their current safety and stability.

Besides, it wasn't his fault that she was absolutely fascinated with him. Around Enzo, she was starting to feel like a teenager with an outsized crush she couldn't handle. As he had reminded her, she was no longer a teenager and she knew that she *should* have better control of her feelings. Especially so soon after her misjudgement of Ritchie's character, she affixed with regret. But perhaps, she thought, with Enzo it was literally a pure sexual attraction sort of a thing and hitting her all the harder because she had never experienced reactions that powerful with anyone else. It was even possible that that was why everything in the bedroom had been a disaster with Ritchie, because she hadn't been sufficiently attracted to her ex from the start. Whichever, she knew she wanted to know and running away from that attraction was foolish when she had still to live in the same house with Enzo.

'I'll do it. Glasgow?'

'We're flying up. I have a business meeting with Robinson first and then I'll pick you up at the hotel and we'll go to lunch at their home the next day.'

'I can wear the same dress I wore last night.'

'No, you can't. They're a very traditional couple

and they don't do anything flash. If you have a rea-
sonable outfit of your own, it will do fine,' he advanced.

'That's a relief,' Skye told him cheerfully. 'I didn't
want you to have to buy me anything more.'

'You really need to be greedier around me,' Enzo
complained. 'I'm used to buying stuff for women.'

'Well, you're not buying stuff for me. It's…just
uncomfortable,' she explained with a wry shake of
her blonde curly head as Shona clasped her knees and
she lifted her baby sister onto her lap. 'You can't mix
as equals when one person is doing all the giving.'

'It hasn't bothered any other woman in my life.'

'You've been involved with the wrong kind of
women, then.'

Enzo didn't know a polite way of telling her that
she sounded like his grandmother, and there was no
polite way of saying that casual sex in return for his
expected generosity went with the same territory
even though nobody was crude enough to state the
fact. So, he said nothing, merely watched her steadily
from beneath long black curling eyelashes, dark eyes
flashing gold as the morning sunlight lit them.

Now she wanted to kill him for the length and
lushness of his eyelashes, Skye conceded, wondering in some desperation when she would return to
sanity and calm again. In Enzo's presence she was
all of a twitter like some stage maiden aunt.

'So, when's this trip taking place?' she prompted.

'We'll fly up Friday and be back by Saturday evening.' With that casual conclusion, Enzo vaulted upright. 'I'll see you tonight.'

'If Mavis comes in back in time, I'll be able to go shopping on my own,' Skye said with relief. 'I won't need to bother your security team.'

'No, they must still accompany you.' Enzo had stilled in the doorway, his lean, darkly handsome features taut. 'Unless your ex is in police custody, you're not safe. Paola spotted him sitting in a car in a layby just up the road yesterday. He's persistent and I don't want you taking any unnecessary risks until he's off the streets.'

Skye paled at the news that Ritchie had been spotted nearby and swallowed the thickness in her throat. The prospect of the complete freedom she longed to reclaim shrank again because, even though she didn't want to admit it, she *was* scared of Ritchie. A shiver ran down her spine at the confirmation that he knew where she was living and that the day before he could have been *that* close to them.

'I'll see you later.' Enzo's firm footsteps sounded in the hall.

'Enzo going?' Brodie prompted in his little voice.

'I'll be home later,' Enzo repeated for her little brother's benefit.

She had only finished cleaning up the kitchen when the bell went. A delivery man handed her a big bouquet of flowers. 'Who's it for?' she asked.

'Skye Davison.'

She retreated indoors with the red roses and looked for a vase in the kitchen. Who on earth would send her flowers? Enzo?

Without hesitation she phoned him because she had to know one way or another. 'Did you send me flowers?' she queried as soon as she heard his deep voice.

At his end of the phone, Enzo frowned reflectively. With the sole exception of his grandmother, he had never sent a woman flowers in his life. 'No. I'm not really a flower-giving sort of guy with women,' he admitted, feeling strangely uncomfortable at making that statement while wondering who the hell had sent her a bouquet.

'Then that means Ritchie sent them. You see, there was no card with them,' she responded tensely. 'Sorry for disturbing you at work.'

And she was gone before he could muster his thoughts into a better response. He groaned out loud. Her beast of an ex was sending her flowers. What a creep the guy was! Later he could not comprehend what he did next because he summoned his PA and ordered flowers for Skye. One of those extravagant wildflower-type arrangements, he described vaguely, instinctively shying away from the romantic intent inherent in sending roses and the like.

Two hours later, Ritchie's roses dispatched to the bin because the sight of them made her flesh crawl,

Skye had a second delivery. A magnificent artistic bouquet was brought in by Paola, who was wreathed in unexpected smiles.

'From the boss,' she announced with deep satisfaction, as if Enzo had trekked through the Amazon jungle to acquire them in some great praiseworthy feat.

Skye texted him.

Enzo, you shouldn't have, but the flowers are really beautiful, thank you.

And Enzo smiled. Well, he had only done it to take her mind off the creep's stratagems, he assured himself, and Skye was far too sensible and practical not to appreciate that there was nothing romantic about the gesture.

The post came in the afternoon. A letter tumbled out of the usual pile of brochures, addressed to some previous occupant of the property, and her heart almost stopped dead when she saw the envelope and her own name because she recognised Ritchie's very distinctive copperplate handwriting immediately and turned pale as milk.

'What is it?' Alana asked.

'A letter from Ritchie,' Skye told her, dropping it on the kitchen table for the younger woman to see.

'Bin it,' her more outspoken sister advised.

'No, I can't do that. I have to open it and if there's

threats in it, I'll have to take it to the police and hand it over and tell the solicitor.' Skye collapsed down on a chair.

'It would be really dumb of him to write down threats. Is he that stupid?'

'I don't want to open it,' Skye admitted dully. 'It just rakes it all up again and plunges me back into what a pathetic mistake I made with him.'

'Ask Paola to check it first. She's a really tough lady,' Alana said admiringly. 'I've signed up for a martial arts class starting after Christmas purely from seeing her in action in that car park with Ritchie. It was so cool.'

'Involving Paola would be gutless. This is *my* responsibility,' Skye declared, lifting a knife off the table where they had had their lunch to slit open the envelope.

She read Ritchie's letter with a sinking heart and a growing sense of disbelief. There was no expression of regret, no admission of fault beyond a reference to her 'fall' and his apparent hope that she had recovered and *calmed down*. It infuriated her almost as much as it intimidated her and when she read to the end and realised that he was trying to get her to meet up with him, her tummy turned over queasily at even the suggestion.

She tossed the letter over to her sister. 'He's trying to get me to agree to see him.'

'Of course, he is. He'll be wanting you to drop

those assault charges. He's going to lose his job and may well go to prison,' Alana pointed out. 'Have you "calmed down"?'

'Not in the slightest. I'll never forget or forgive what he did to me.'

'So, will you agree to tell Enzo I'm in for that assistant night-shift manager promotion at the Blackthorn?' Her sister was returning to an earlier conversation.

'I don't think it would be fair,' Skye parried a second time.

Alana grimaced. 'He owns the blasted place! It would mean nothing to him!'

'He's done me enough favours,' Skye countered.

Alana rolled her eyes. 'You're the one doing *him* favours. Fake girlfriend? Trip to Glasgow?'

'Alana, look at what he's had done to Mavis. She's transformed,' Skye argued. 'He must've spent hundreds of pounds on that car.'

'I reckon thousands,' her sister opined. 'It didn't even look that good when Mum bought it ten years ago.'

Enzo arrived home to an empty house and was greeted rapturously only by Sparky.

'Skye and her sister went out shopping,' Paola reported. 'Antonio and Matteo are with them.'

Enzo reheated the meal left for him in the microwave and wondered if Skye really thought he was stupid enough to need the step-by-step instructions she had left for him, but, on another level, he was telling himself that he should be relieved that Skye was absent. Their relationship—and even the word threatened a man who didn't have relationships—had a weird lack of boundaries and he *had* sent her those showy flowers on prominent display in the hall. She *worked* for him, he reminded himself fiercely. She was an employee even if she didn't feel like one, any more than the kids and the dog felt like an employee's dependants. He had got too close to her, become too involved. Intelligence warned him that he should pull back. Having eaten, he went into the room he was using as an office and stubbornly ignored the sounds of Skye and her siblings returning home.

Skye couldn't sleep that night. She had wanted to see Enzo and she hadn't seen him and then had warned herself that she had no need to see him either. The *clingy* housekeeper, knocking on the door with an offer of supper? No, that was not a label she sought. She grimaced.

Around one in the morning, weary of tossing and turning, she went down to the kitchen to have a cup of tea and dug Ritchie's letter out of her bag to have another look at it. She refused to be scared of him or of anything he had written. Unhappily, all those nasty little jabs about how overly emotional she could be, how she jumped to conclusions, how she always thought the worst in situations and dramatised herself washed over her afresh and knocked her flat. Rereading the letter had not been a good idea, she acknowledged. Even mulling over his criticisms of her after he had violently assaulted her was crazy.

Enzo heard Skye heading downstairs and worried that something was amiss. He climbed out of bed and tugged on a pair of jeans, deeming a T-shirt unnecessary. Barefoot, he descended the stairs without a sound and saw Skye sitting at the kitchen table, her head buried in her folded arms, her narrow shoulders shaking.

'What's wrong?' Enzo demanded, striding over to her, registering that she was quietly crying.

'Go away,' she told him hoarsely. 'I'm having a mini breakdown and I don't need an audience!'

'What's this?' Enzo lifted the letter off the table. 'He had the nerve to write you a *letter* after what he did?' he bit out incredulously.

Enzo read it and rolled his eyes, tossing it back down on the table while Skye mopped her eyes and struggled to regain control. 'You can tell he's abusive simply by the stuff he writes. He beat you up and he's finding fault with you!'

'I know. How could I have been foolish enough to move in with a man like that?' she gasped, stricken, and leapt out of her chair to rush over and put on the kettle. 'Do you want something to drink?'

'Water will do me.'

Enzo breathed in deep and slow, hating that sense of being out of his depth, but there was no use pretending that he was experienced at comforting distressed women when he had always avoided distressed women like the plague. As he followed her across the spacious kitchen, he rested both hands on her slender shoulders in an effort to ground her.

'You didn't know what he was like until you moved in with him. People don't wear their secrets, flaws and kinks like badges. They keep up a front to lure you in until you trust them. But you're not to blame. He's a weirdo and I'm dropping that letter into the police tomorrow morning.'

'Thanks,' she muttered. 'But I'm just so angry with myself.'

'Try being angry with *him*! How dare he send you flowers and write to you after assaulting you?' Enzo framed in a raw undertone. 'Call your solicitor and update him about this. I'm quite sure that the police will have warned your ex to stay well away from you and now he's harassing you.'

Skye spun round with a moisture-beaded glass of water for him. He set it down on the counter behind her and stared down at her with intense dark golden eyes. 'You shouldn't be crying about that bastard, you should be celebrating the fact that you escaped him!'

'That letter upset me. I'll get over it. And I wasn't crying about *him*, I was crying about how stupid

I was to trust him and now the kids have had all this upheaval…'

'Your siblings are perfectly happy here.'

'Enzo…working here is only a staging post because it's temporary. I have to think of the future and we'll be moving on *again*.'

His hands slid down from her shoulders to her hands. 'Take a deep breath and give yourself time to recover from what happened to you first. It's much too soon for you to be freaking out about the future.'

'I wish it was, but I've already been here two weeks and in another six weeks you may be gone,' she pointed out, frantically striving not to look at his bare chest.

Half naked, there was so much of him, an expanse of bronzed hair-roughened muscular flesh that any woman would have gawped at. He towered over her with his taut abs, well-developed biceps and a flat stomach framed by that fabled vee of lean muscle leading down to his hips. Perspiration broke out on her short upper lip as she looked up at him, connecting with stormy dark-as-night eyes, beautiful eyes, changeable according to mood, she had long since learned. The tension in the atmosphere was stifling her ability to breathe. She sucked in air a little desperately.

Enzo ran a long finger along the lower line of her lips, feeling that soft pillowy mouth he wanted under his and fighting that instinct with all his might. Holding her breath tight, in a spirit of unfamiliar daring, Skye lifted her hand and shakily traced the waistband of his jeans. He was as aroused as she was. The prominent bulge below the denim assured her of that and it made her feel almost light-headed with satisfaction, vindicating the feminine power that Ritchie had assured her she didn't have. One of the many insults he had hurled while she'd lain on that floor in terror had been that she was sexless and frigid, useless to any normal man.

'You don't want this,' Enzo told her hoarsely.

'What I don't want,' she whispered unevenly, 'is another man making *my* choices for me.'

'I'm trying to protect you,' Enzo gritted between clenched teeth, because with every breath she drew her small breasts stirred beneath the thin pyjama top she wore, the peaks of her nipples indenting the cloth, and he wanted to grab her, ravish her, do everything his raging libido demanded that he do. His lean hands clenched into knotted fists by his side.

'I can protect myself,' Skye argued, spinning round to walk away, chin lifted against rejection, determined not to betray that another ego-squashing wound had been inflicted.

Enzo ground something out in explosive Italian and then lifted her up against him to set her down on the table edge, standing back again, deliberately not crowding her. 'You need a friend right now, *not* a lover.'

The ease with which he lifted her off her feet and set her down again struck her as ridiculously sexy. He was strong but he didn't use that strength against her. 'There's nothing wrong with a friend with benefits,' Skye heard herself say.

And that declaration disagreed with every moral tenet and ideal Skye had ever cherished and she knew it did. But she wanted Enzo, and she was willing to fib because she knew that it would only ever be a passing thing with him and that there was no other way of being with him. Either she accepted that, or she didn't. But right now, after her life had fallen in round her ears with every hope and expectation destroyed, she was struggling to find her feet in a new world and somehow being desired by Enzo made her feel better, so much better she couldn't believe it.

'I'm not sure I can believe that you mean that,' Enzo murmured, searching dark golden eyes compelling hers. 'I was very sure you were a white-picket-fence girl with a church at the end of the drive.'

Skye flushed to the very roots of her hair because Enzo had already had her labelled and he was entirely correct with his estimate. She had wanted love, she had wanted a wedding, she had wanted everything perfect, only to discover that life was not perfect any more than men were or even she was. And now she was in a new place, ready to try something different, something more, something much bolder than her usual choices.

'I'm changing my outlook.'

Enzo rested his mesmeric dark golden eyes on her hot face. 'But I don't want you doing that just for me. I don't want to hurt you. With me, it's sex and a good time. There's nothing else on offer,' he spelt out curtly.

Skye gulped because that sounded so harsh and hurtful and risky and she wasn't a risk-taker, never had been. It sounded like a devil's bargain for a young woman who believed in love, who was already getting more attached than she should be to the man in front of her. She swallowed hard, her hands gripping the edge of the table as she sat there. 'I understand.'

'I don't think I'd be much good at anything deeper,' Enzo breathed in a roughened undertone.

But he had a huge heart even though he hid it to the very best of his ability, Skye reflected, confused by him and by all the conflicting messages he gave her. His actions with her had taught her to trust in that heart of his even though he was not emotionally available to her. He could be warm and gentle one moment, then cold and hard the next. He was unfathomable, unpredictable, everything she had once avoided in a man. Her brain screamed that she would be making a mistake but thought had no control over instinct and every instinct she possessed drew her to Enzo.

'You deserve a much nicer guy,' Enzo added, still stubbornly holding back.

Skye looked up at him and laughed because she couldn't help it. She stretched out her arms to tug him closer, hands travelling up his taut spine to his shoulders and even sitting on the table it was a stretch for her. 'Shut up, Enzo…please stop talking and just kiss me…'

CHAPTER SIX

ENZO LOOKED DOWN into those entrancing lilac eyes of hers and all his disciplined restraint evaporated in the same moment. His hands rose of their own volition to cup her triangular face, long fingers slowly spearing into her soft mop of curls.

Her face was already so familiar to him that he wondered sometimes if she reminded him of someone, but she was too individual to be a copy of anyone else. The only woman he had ever known who had breakfast with him without make-up on. The only woman who finished a phone call even faster than he did. The only woman, who seemed to see him for who he was rather than what he possessed and who treated him accordingly, just as if he was the same as everyone else. And best of all, Skye had not a clue how special it was for someone like him to be treated as though he was no one special either. In much the same way, he registered, he had not a clue why he found that so appealing a trait.

'Enzo...' Skye urged, every fibre of her being tensely awaiting the slow descent of his lips onto hers, his lips brushing back and forth over hers, so gentle, so stimulating as he gathered her up off the table like a doll and literally welded her to every muscular line of his long, hard body. Every sensitive spot she possessed squirmed with delight at that full contact and she gasped. It was like the kiss in the car, like sticking her finger in an electric socket, like a tidal wave engulfing her. Excitement rolled through her in a heady surge and made her wonder if she could be quite normal in such an overreaction.

When she surfaced, she was in Enzo's bedroom with no recollection of the journey upstairs. 'You *carried* me up here?' she exclaimed as he settled her down on the tumbled bed.

'You don't weigh much more than your little brother. It was hardly an extraordinary feat.' Enzo laughed.

And now here they were in the bedroom where the bonfire of her best hopes had previously burned into dreary ash. Apprehension leapt through her. 'There's just one thing I don't like...the choking thing,' she muttered uncomfortably, needing to put that out there but cringing at the necessity of saying it.

Comprehension gripped Enzo and he mentally cursed the male who had put that nervous, anxious look on her flushed face. 'I'm not into that sort of stuff. In fact, I'm pretty vanilla in my tastes. Nothing to frighten the horses, as my grandmother would say.'

'That's a very English saying,' she remarked, relief filling her to overflowing.

'My grandmother *is* English. Nonno…my grandfather…met her when she was a chalet girl at a ski lodge when they were both very young. Against everybody's wishes, they married and they're still together.'

'That's why your English is so good.'

'Probably.' Enzo could see the nerves infiltrating her again, her skin taut across her cheekbones, eyes downcast. 'Do you mind me asking if your ex was your first lover?'

Skye nodded silent confirmation.

'So, practically a virgin on my terms,' Enzo teased as he unzipped his jeans and kicked them aside to come down beside her on the rucked bed. 'I may not be able to offer you for ever, but I can show you pleasure and, hopefully, a little fun.'

He didn't have a shy bone in his body. Why would he have? she asked herself, scanning his near godlike physical perfection. He was all bronzed, hair-roughened vitality and virility. He was also primed for action and there was definitely more of him than she was accustomed to dealing with. She lay back on the bed, trying not to feel like a human sacrifice, wondering for a moment what insanity had persuaded her that she ought to try again to see if intimacy was any different with Enzo.

'Look on the bright side,' Enzo whispered, leaning over her with unvarnished cool. 'If you don't like it with me either, you don't ever have to do it again.'

'I suppose that's a good point,' she said, a little breathless at him being that close.

She sat up again, almost knocking him back, nervous tension making her jerky and indecisive. She peeled her pyjama top over her head, snaked her hips free of the shorts, flung them on the floor, lay back down again and found Enzo staring down at her with wondering amusement brimming in his gaze.

'What?' she said flatly.

'You're so obviously in this "let's get this over as fast as possible" mode,' he proffered. 'And that's not how I operate.'

Skye ignored him to slide beneath the duvet, too self-conscious about her lack of sexy curves to stay naked on top of the bedding.

'Do you think it's possible for you to switch off your brain and relax for a moment?'

'Doubt it.'

'You're not allowed to bail on me as soon as it's over, either,' Enzo warned her, although a quick departure had never bothered him with any other woman because he never stayed the whole night with anyone. But he already knew that it would be different with Skye, that he had *one* chance and he had to go for it and make the most he could out of it.

'Why not?'

'Because that's not what I want…perfunctory sex, brief and superficial.'

'I thought that's what you specialised in. Isn't that what womanisers do?'

'What would you know about womanisers?' Enzo enquired as he slid in beside her, sudden heat burning down her right side, making her shiver in reaction.

'Nothing,' she admitted.

'Well, there you are. It's not all about scoring for me, at least not with you.'

'I'm sure you say that to all your women,' Skye told him huffily. 'I don't need that sort of reassurance. I'm perfectly happy just to be here…for *one* night.'

'And all the more precious for it,' Enzo husked, claiming her parted lips with his warm, hungry mouth, stealing the very breath from her lungs as honeyed warmth spread through her lower body, driving off the chill of nerves that had been spreading through her.

'Enzo… I—'

'Shush,' he hummed against her parted lips. 'I'm not going to do anything you don't want to do and the minute you say stop, I *stop*. You can trust me.'

Skye drew in a quivering breath, feeling reassured. 'All right.'

'It will be better than all right; it will be fantastic because we have explosive chemistry.'

'Is that so?'

'*Sì*...that means yes.'

'I know that! You're always spluttering Italian when you're not thinking about it,' she told him.

And Enzo laughed and thought how unusual it was for him to laugh with a woman in bed, never mind have a conversation. He lifted his dark tousled head and stared down at her in the lamplight and used a long finger to trace her fine brows, her delicate cheekbones and the soft pink cushion of her swollen lips. 'You're beautiful.'

And she almost argued with him but bit it back, assuming it was standard for him to say that sort of thing, but that didn't mean that she had to be clumsy about receiving a compliment, did it? As far as she was concerned the only beautiful individual in the room was Enzo with his classic bone structure, dark deep-set eyes and that particular rare smile on his lips that hinted that he didn't have a care in the world.

'You're so warm,' she told him with a grin. 'As good as an electric blanket.'

'Livelier, I hope, *piccolo mio*.'

Still smiling, Enzo shaped a dainty breast with a hunger he was fiercely striving to restrain. He brushed away the bedding only to discover that she was inadvertently holding onto it. He detached her from the duvet like a man making the first move to open a box containing a fascinating puzzle. He bent over her, the apprehension in her wide eyes clenching something painful inside his broad chest. In all his life no woman had ever looked at him with that degree of anxiety and so he kissed her and he kissed her for a very, very long time, sliding against her, dipping his tongue in the tender interior of her mouth with a little flick and a promise that began to ignite something low in her pelvis that Skye had never felt before.

All sorts of unfamiliar sensations began to shimmy through Skye and demolish her tension to replace it with a tension of a different type. She grew less worried about Enzo hurting or embarrassing her and more concerned with what he would do next, which, she dimly registered, was a lot healthier an attitude. Her fingers crept up over his stubbled jaw into his luxuriant black hair. It felt so good to finally touch him again and so strange to realise that she who had come to detest physical contact with one man could be so different with another.

Enzo stroked a taut pink nipple while toying with its twin. He captured the swollen peak with his mouth and dallied there, teasing and sucking and tasting until the burst of warmth being created in Skye's pelvis rose into a flame, making her push her hips down into the mattress and writhe, unable to lie still.

'I want us both to enjoy this, *piccolo mio*,' Enzo

intoned when Skye sent him a winging glance of impatience. 'It's not likely to be over in five minutes.'

'I didn't say a word!' she protested shakily.

But Skye was stubborn for all her diminutive size, Enzo reckoned. It shone out of her character. She was the woman who had taken on her vulnerable siblings in spite of the reality that that weight and size of responsibility had made her life much more difficult. She was the woman irritated with him for paying for all the food in the kitchen even while she was staying there with her little brother and sister. She was used to independence and hated relying on other people. Her hand ran down over his chest to skim a long, powerful thigh and his mind went momentarily blank.

He returned her hand concisely to the mattress. 'Tonight, it's my show.'

'You're a control freak.'

'No, I know I'm on trial and I need a clear head,' Enzo countered smooth as glass.

'I did not say you were on trial.'

'But we both know I am,' he replied unanswerably.

As Skye compressed her lips, still struggling to control herself and her responses, Enzo kissed her again with passionate urgency and why it was so important to hold the line then escaped her. Enzo was very good at kissing, so good that before he could regroup and address his attention elsewhere, she grabbed him back to her, her own hunger for his mouth coming out of nowhere at her and startling her.

'I'm doing okay,' Enzo drawled thickly, all confidence and unshakeable control, as he kissed a haphazard trail down over her midriff.

'Did I say that?'

'In bed your body speaks for you,' Enzo purred, entirely preoccupied by her smooth satiny soft skin and every tiny revealing twitch of her slender hips.

'Enzo…' she gasped on a long, broken sigh as he traced the heart of her with his fingers and his tongue.

Skye had never indulged in that particular pursuit before and her body's fiery reaction took her very much by surprise. Enzo was discovering sensitivities even she had not known she possessed. When he ran the tip of his tongue along the line of her inner thigh, she almost spontaneously combusted at the surge of heat that began to warm her up from the inside out. Indeed, being in bed with Enzo, it was almost impossible for her to think with any clarity. She would start a thought and then he would do something that tore her every expectation up and shook her from head to toe.

He traced her, he stroked her, he explored her. And little tremors of response began to run through Skye like a river threatening to burst its banks and overflow. He had trapped her because she could no more have persuaded herself to get out of that bed than she could have stopped breathing. And it was a revelation to her that sex could feel so intense and so powerful that it suppressed every other response.

The clenching low in her pelvis led to an inner tightness like a knot low in her tummy and she couldn't stay still then, she became insanely conscious of Enzo's big hands clamped to her hips. She twisted and squirmed and suddenly that ball of heat inside her just mushroomed up out of her in an earth-shaking climax that left her quivering and in shock in the aftermath.

'Did you like that?' Enzo whispered.

And that fast, she wanted to slap him for his nerve. 'It was okay,' she told him unevenly.

Skye watched him don a condom, all of an unexpected quiver inside herself because she was wanting something she had learned not to want and it unnerved her. He slid over her, all male, hot and demanding and, for a moment, she simply tuned him out, refused to think, refused to feel.

Enzo claimed her lips in a long, drugging kiss. 'There you are again, *piccolo mio*,' he remarked, dark eyes gleaming gold, and she reddened, registering that he had noted her withdrawal.

Comparisons were utterly distasteful to her but it was different, everything was different from past experience. Enzo sank into the slippery welcome of her and sent a jolt of arousal travelling through her lower body. From there, and to her astonishment, it only became more riveting in the most delicious of ways. In fact, she responded with all the enthusiasm of a new convert, eager to learn and progress. Every movement of his body into hers delivered a jolt of arousal beyond anything she had experienced. Her ability to reason was interrupted by the sheer intensity of excitement that began to grip her. The clench of her internal muscles meshed with growing heat and a powerful wave of renewed response engulfed her before she was flung breathless and gasping into a second climax that absolutely wiped her out.

'Was I a hero or a zero?' Enzo enquired with a flippancy that set her teeth on edge.

Skye sat up. 'I think you know.'

He grabbed her arm. 'Where are you going?'

'Back to my room. I'm sure your one-nighters,' she commented with a flippancy to match his own lack of tact, 'don't stay either—'

'The difference is that I *want* you to stay,' Enzo cut in, tugging her down to him again.

Disconcerted, Skye lay back down as he brought her close and wrapped both arms round her. In truth she was very tired. Her days were always long and started early, as was the norm with young children to care for. She was mentally listing all the reasons why she should return to her own bed when she fell asleep.

Enzo woke to find a two-year-old kneeling beside him.

'Dood morning,' Brodie said with a huge grin. 'You dot Skye wif you?'

Enzo laughed and nudged Skye awake because he couldn't get up naked. Of course, she was naked too, he realised, and he leant out of bed to reach for the PJs she had discarded the night before and shoved them in her general direction. Quicker than him, Skye made herself presentable, sliding out of bed to gather up Brodie, who was full of beans and chattering away as she took him out of the bedroom.

Enzo was downstairs, showered, shaved and fully clothed in one of his business suits in record time, only to discover his breakfast had been laid once again in the dining room. He suppressed a groan, feeling as though he had been sent into exile. Once more, Skye was imposing distance between them and he didn't like it. After all, they had had a great time together. Why would she now start treating him as though nothing had changed?

Skye bashed around the kitchen, working fast on the breakfast clean-up because she had signed Brodie up to a new, more convenient playgroup and she would drop him off and then go shopping with Shona.

'Zozo...' Shona framed brightly, pausing in her greeting crawl to the doorway where Enzo hovered.

Skye turned red as fire even before she turned

around to face him as she had hoped to avoid doing. What was she playing at? She had had her first ever and probably *last* ever one-night stand. That wasn't her and would probably never be her but the benefit was, she told herself, that she was now free of the fears Ritchie had cursed her with. She had had a fabulous time with Enzo but in truth she was somewhat ashamed of having taken that freedom to share a bed with him. Her book of rules had no room for uncommitted sex and now she was free of her ex, she had no plans to change her value system.

'You're not speaking to me,' Enzo gathered as he bent down and swept up Shona, who was now clinging hopefully to his legs. 'But *you* are, aren't you? Even if I have to be called Zozo!' he teased, swinging her high up into the air so that the little girl laughed in delight.

'Of course, I'm speaking to you,' Skye responded in a rattled undertone. 'I hope I'm not that childish.'

'But you're avoiding me as if we did something shameful,' he pointed out.

Skye burned so hot she was surprised she didn't flame under her skin because that particular adjective made her think about some timeless dark space of the night when he had turned to her, or she had turned to him—she didn't honestly know which of them had been responsible—and once again they had made love with a passion that still mortified her. In fact, she hadn't been able to get enough of him and that awareness *did* make it a huge challenge to treat Enzo as an employer.

'I work for you,' she reminded him chokily.

'Don't hold *that* against me. Not much I can do about it,' he traded levelly. 'Keep it separate.'

'I *can't*,' Skye framed woodenly.

Lean, darkly handsome features taut, Enzo murmured, 'Are you still accompanying me to Glasgow?'

'I promised. Yes.'

Enzo nodded in silence and then laid Shona gently down on the floor again. She looked up at him with disappointed eyes. 'I'll see you later,' he told her.

Skye breathed in deep and slow as the front door slammed shut on Enzo's departure. She was doing the right thing…she was doing the right thing, she told herself urgently. Step away, pull back, don't bounce into another relationship straight after the hard lesson that had been Ritchie, especially when the very word 'relationship' might bring Enzo out in a cold sweat. But she should not even be thinking of him. She had to be stable and sensible for the children's sake and for the foreseeable future that meant no men.

CHAPTER SEVEN

A FEW DAYS LATER, Skye rested back in a reclining white leather seat of incredible opulence on Enzo's private jet.

For all the attention Enzo was paying her, though, she might as well not have been onboard. Attention had, nevertheless, been showered on Enzo by the glamorous blonde beauty acting as stewardess. In fact, so noticeable was the blonde's interest in her boss that Skye was embarrassed witnessing her sultry smiles and her habit of bending over to serve him with rather too many shirt buttons undone. To give him his due, however, Enzo had ignored the display and the underwritten invitation.

And why was she thinking about it anyway? Enzo had been working on his laptop throughout the journey, brief though the flight to Glasgow was to be. Skye had no grounds for complaint: nobody was more conscious of that fact. She had reminded him of the boundaries of their working relationship, and he had stuck scrupulously to those limits ever since. He had still, nonetheless, continued to play with the kids and acknowledge the dog.

Skye? Only Skye was now out in the cold. She got the occasional murmured thanks when she put a plate in front of him and absolutely no personal chat. Be careful what you wish for, she reflected ruefully, because you might just get it and discover that you didn't like it the smallest bit.

Alana had suggested that she was acting like an idiot. She had even hinted that she thought that Skye *could* be punishing Enzo for Ritchie's sins...*as if*! But then Lorenzo Durante had no bigger fan than her sister, who believed the sun rose and set on him because he had come to her family's rescue that night by the side of the road.

Alana had been very much looking forward to an evening with her little brother and sister in the comfort of the old house. In a sudden passion of regret and confusion over her troubled state of mind, Skye wished she were with her sister, but as soon as she glanced across the aisle at Enzo, she knew she was lying to herself to save face.

Enzo looked amazing in a dark pinstripe suit teamed with a fashionable royal-blue shirt and paler silk tie and it was a challenge for her to keep her eyes off him. What right had she to resent the steward- ess trying to flirt with him? No right whatsoever, when she had directly warned him off. It was little wonder though that Enzo Durante had a reputation with women. He drew her sex like bees to a honeypot. With his height, athletic build and lean bronzed classic features, he was extravagantly good-looking. Even his voice, that husky purr he used in bed, had made her very toes curl! Wreathed in blushes and mortified heat at that last, far too intimate recollection, Skye lifted the magazine on her lap and attempted to read it.

Skye definitely didn't like the stewardess flirting with him, Enzo ruminated. Was that a dog-in-the-manger attitude? And why did he care anyway? For several years he had had the vague suspicion that *all* the women he met were totally interchangeable in looks, clothing and personality, but Skye stood out from the crowd for him and had from the outset, though he still had to work out why. It wasn't healthy to be brooding over one of the very few rejections he had ever received. It was done and dusted, *over*. As always, he remained free as a bird and that had always been his preference. So, what if it had been an incredible night? His preoccupation, his ongoing interest in her, was beginning to exasperate him.

They passed through the busy airport where Enzo attracted a good deal of fascinated feminine scrutiny. A luxurious limousine awaited them outside and Skye slid into it, feeling like a stranger in a foreign land and, much as she had felt on the luxury private jet, poorly dressed for such surroundings and out of place. The hotel, however, was even more intimidating from the moment they were greeted by name by their personal concierge in the echoing marble foyer, which contained various groups of clearly wealthy people, the women with perfect hair, clad in the subtle gleam of expensive jewellery and the latest fashions. Into the lift they went and then they were shown into a vast suite with sleek modern furniture and an elegant décor, other doors leading off to bedrooms.

While Skye was packing her small case, she had actually wondered if Enzo would somehow inveigle her into sharing a room with him, but evidently that was *not* a scenario she needed to worry about. It was impossible to explain why Enzo choosing to go to the opposite extreme and proving that he was honourable should make her feel slightly depressed. Her face flushed, she went into the room designated as hers by the concierge and began to unpack. Beyond the doorway she could hear Enzo talking on the phone in Italian, the lyrical rise and fall of his dark drawl, the syllables sliding softly against each other striking her as outrageously sensual. So, you still have a bad case of the hots for your employer, Skye conceded. Stop it, just *stop it*.

'I'm afraid there's been a change in our itinerary,' Enzo announced from the doorway. 'Robinson has asked me to view a company he's thinking of buying and, because it's close to his home, he has invited us to stay there and dine with them tonight instead.

And I may have underestimated Robinson's lifestyle because, apparently, he lives in a *castle*.'

'Oh, my goodness.' Skye grimaced, thinking of the plain trousers and sweater she had decided would do for the non-fancy lunch date. 'My outfit won't pass muster at dinner in a castle!'

Enzo shrugged a broad shoulder. 'Relax. I'll get that sorted now.'

'How?' Skye immediately bristled, her small figure going rigid. 'I don't want you spending any more money on me, Enzo!'

Enzo raised a perfectly shaped ebony brow at her raised tone of voice. 'We're only talking about a few props to aid the fake-girlfriend charade,' he said very drily, as if she were making a fuss about nothing.

'It's not that simple,' Skye protested.

'It's exactly that simple but, by all means, give away anything I buy you to a charity shop afterwards, if it makes you feel better,' Enzo countered in the same flat, laconic tone. 'Is that it?'

In frustration, Skye whirled away from him and stationed herself beside the window. Her teeth were gritted. 'You don't understand.'

'Try me.' Enzo heaved a sigh, while striving not to notice how shapely her legs were below the skirt she had worn to travel in. A memory of sliding between those slender thighs did not help and he frowned, the throb at his groin offending him. Where was his self-discipline? He was furious with himself, furi-

ous with her for making what he deemed to be a fuss
about inconsequential stuff. What the hell did what
she wore and who paid for it have to do with anything? How could that be important?

'You buying me clothes, it makes me uncomfortable because Ritchie controlled what I wore while
I was with him,' she explained reluctantly. 'It made
me feel like he owned me.'

'I'm not your ex. I know I don't own you. I have
no influence over what you do or where you go and
you know it. We're in companion territory, *not* relationship territory,' he reminded her with strong
emphasis. 'Even so, if you want to wear your own
clothes and risk feeling underdressed this evening,
that is your choice to make.'

Inwardly, Skye cringed at the prospect of being
underdressed at a *castle*. 'Possibly I was a bit hasty
in my objections,' she muttered grudgingly.

'I thought you would see it that way,' Enzo parried smoothly, relieved that common sense was once
again in control of her. 'Now let's get this show on
the road.'

Suitable outfits, she learned, would be brought
to the hotel suite for her viewing while she could
use the hotel beauty spa for any grooming requirements she felt necessary. And with that casual conclusion, Enzo apologised for the change of plan that
their host's new itinerary had forced on them and
departed with his luggage. She would not see him

again until she arrived at the castle and she didn't much fancy arriving at a castle alone without Enzo to hide behind.

Enzo left the hotel feeling thoroughly dissatisfied and not quite sure why that should be the case. He was being sensible, he assured himself fiercely. He had got badly hurt in his one and only relationship and he refused to do anything like that to Skye. The more distance there was between them, the safer she would be.

The stylist and her assistant with a rail of glamorous clothes and bags of accessories arrived with Skye within the hour. She supposed that someone like Enzo always got top service of that nature and he took it for granted in a way she never would because he had, it seemed, grown up accustomed to such advantages.

Having picked a dress, she noted that nothing had a price tag attached and, wondering if that omission was at Enzo's instigation, she also selected shoes with a heel because she had only brought flats. That achieved, she booked a late afternoon appointment for her hair at the hotel spa and was wondering what to do next when Paola arrived to inform her that she and a car were at her disposal.

'I'm starting to feel like an overnight princess,' she joked with the older woman.

'Nothing wrong with that,' Paola told her with a

smile. 'Have you any idea what you would like to do with the rest of the day?'

And Skye had a very good idea. She had watched a programme on television about the famous stately home, Dumfries House, saved for the public by the King's intervention before his ascension to the throne. True, it was a winter day, but it was sunny and dry, and she knew that she would still enjoy the house and gardens.

As the estate was only forty miles from Glasgow, she and Paola decided to enjoy lunch there at the Coach House Café. They were just walking out of the house with its fabulous Chippendale collection of furniture into the gardens when she rang Alana to ask if she was comfortable staying at the house with the children.

Alana sighed. 'Yes, but I've been too angry after Ritchie's visit to relax.'

Skye froze in dismay. 'Ritchie came to the *house*?'

'This morning Yes, I should think your application for that non-molestation order will be easily granted now. I'm surprised Paola didn't tell you about it,' her sister rattled on. 'She was marvellous and called the police and he was arrested. Apparently, he'd been suspended and he was trying to blame you for it. He's also very worked up about you living in Enzo's home. I was grateful you weren't here. He's put you through enough.'

When Skye came off her phone, Paola gave her

a rueful smile of understanding. 'The boss asked me not to tell you. He didn't want you to be upset.'

Skye nodded acceptance of the older woman's loyalty to her employer and resolved to tackle Enzo on her own. Of course, there was nothing she could have done to protect her sister from that visit and clearly Alana had been safe with Paola present. 'So, you only flew up to Scotland this morning?' she said to the other woman.

'Yes.'

'I was incredibly lucky to meet Enzo that night on the road.' Perhaps that was a rather belated appreciation, Skye reflected guiltily. Enzo had gone above and beyond to protect her and the children from Ritchie's confrontations. And in her ignorance, she had rather taken it all for granted, not even considering the costs or inconveniences caused by that level of protection.

'Keeping security on the house and me while Enzo was at work must have left you short-staffed,' Skye surmised lightly.

'The boss brought in more guards from home.'

Determined not to betray how much that information embarrassed her, Skye asked, 'Where in Italy is home?'

'The boss's grandparents live in Tuscany but he's mainly based at an apartment in Rome, although he owns other properties round the world,' Paola told her. 'He inherited some of them from his father.'

'How long have you worked for Enzo?'

'I left the police, trained as a paramedic and became a bodyguard when he was a little boy and I worked for his grandfather. I'm older than I look.' Paola chuckled as Skye glanced at her in surprise.

They passed a very pleasant afternoon wandering round the beautiful gardens before returning to the hotel where Skye went to the spa and then returned to the suite to dress.

Garbed in a dark purple sheath dress worn with toning heels, Skye climbed into the waiting car and found a package on the seat beside her with her name on it. She opened it up and tugged out a jewel case in some dismay to reveal a delicate gold necklace with a glittering diamond-studded star pendant. It was gorgeous. She was supposed to be Enzo's girlfriend. The necklace was only a prop and not something she would be keeping, she told herself as she attached it to her throat.

When the car drove down a long, wooded driveway an hour later and the massive castle with its twin circular towers was revealed, Skye was enormously relieved to see Enzo standing outside the front door with an older man, obviously waiting there in readiness to greet her. Her nerves evaporated and she fairly surged out of the car as he strode across the gravel towards her.

The slender beauty of her in the plain but elegant dress made Enzo smile, particularly when he saw the diamond star twinkling in the lights. He had hoped she would wear it because she ought to have more pretty things, he reasoned absently. From what he had witnessed, he reckoned the little ones got first bite of every financial apple and that she rarely spent on herself. He had not seen her wear a single new item since they had met and, being highly observant, Enzo noticed the fact.

'My word…the castle is huge,' she whispered.

'*Sì*…talk about an underestimation,' Enzo conceded with the slanting easy grin that illuminated his lean, darkly handsome face and her heart jumped inside her, refusing to settle except to a fast pitter-patter as he dropped an arm round her to guide her back towards their host.

Skye discovered that she wanted to nestle into that sheltering arm and it unnerved her. The scent of the cologne he used flared her nostrils, intimate memories tugging at her composure as she was introduced to Robinson Davies, slightly stooped with age but still a hearty man with grey hair and twinkling blue eyes. A step indoors, she met his wife, Alyson, who took over to show Skye to her room.

'You could have brought the children with you,' the tall dark-haired woman told her. 'We had no idea you had a family until Enzo told us. I love children. My grandchildren are teenagers now and it's difficult to organise visits when they're studying at school.'

'Perhaps if we visit again, we'll bring the children.' Skye smiled as warmly as she could, wanting to respond to that friendly hospitality while knowing that she was extremely unlikely ever to meet the woman a second time because, after all, for all her impressive props, she remained only a fake, not a genuine girlfriend.

She was shown into a gorgeous circular bedroom in one of the towers where a fire already burned in the imposing stone fireplace. She adored it and asked all sorts of questions about the history of the building.

'Sadly, it's getting too big for us now and we're thinking of looking for a more manageable retirement home. It was different when we had four children running round the place.'

'Times change,' Skye acknowledged as Alyson departed again.

It was only then that she noticed that Enzo's luggage was in the room as well and she frowned. She was willing to bet that Enzo had not foreseen that development.

Twenty minutes later, he joined her. '*Sì*, we're sharing,' he conceded wryly. 'That surprised me. They're very close with my grandparents and my grandparents would never put an unmarried couple in the same room.'

'I think that could be seen as quite old-fashioned these days...but I'm not criticising your family. Their home, their rules,' Skye hastened to assure him. 'I'm sure we can manage for one night.'

'I'll use the sofa.'

Skye glanced at the majestic wood-framed antique by the wall and laughed in disagreement because, while an impressive piece, it looked as though it would offer all the comfort of a bed of nails. 'No need for such dramatic gestures, Enzo. It's a huge bed. We can share it.'

Some of the tension left Enzo's taut features at her relaxed acceptance. He yanked up a case and opened it to extract a suit bag. 'Do you mind if I use the bathroom first?'

'No. I'm already dressed for the evening.'

He took his change of clothing into the bathroom but before doing so, he made a rather endearing effort to tidy up the tumbled case. 'I'll fix it,' she told him with amusement.

Pre-dinner drinks were served in a comfortable sitting room. Skye settled down with Alyson Davies and the two women discussed her visit to Dumfries House and the gardens there.

'Do you have a garden of your own?'

'No. I've never had a garden.'

'Never?' Enzo broke into their dialogue to query. 'How did you get interested in the great outdoors, then?'

'We always lived in an apartment, but my stepfather had an allotment where he grew all our vegetables,' Skye told them with a smile. 'He allowed me to have a little patch to grow annual flowers every summer.'

'If you don't mind me asking,' Alyson murmured, 'what happened to your real father?'

'Oh, that's a very long story,' Skye declared lightly. 'And not one I'm comfortable sharing outside the family.'

A potentially awkward moment was smoothed over by Skye's warm and ready smile. She was good with people, Enzo acknowledged, would be an asset at business socialising because she didn't have a rude, unkind or pretentious bone in her body. He was starting to see why Skye had more effect on him than other women had. She truly *was* different. And he watched her, even while he talked to his host, noting the pink plumpness of her lower lip, the light glow of her beautiful eyes, the slender shapely legs crossing, one dainty ankle dangling, and his hunger for her mounted, making him tense.

Having promised to allow Alyson and Robinson the chance to give her a grand tour of their walled garden after breakfast the next day, Skye and Enzo headed upstairs to bed.

'Am I allowed to ask about your birth father?' he enquired. 'Feel free to tell me to mind my own business if it's painful.'

'No, it's not painful, just a little too personal to unpack in company. Mum got pregnant with me

when she was at school. My father and her were six-
teen and some people tend to be judgemental about
that,' she explained with a grimace. 'Her parents
threw her out and *his* parents took her in. That lasted
for about two years, long enough for Mum to conceive Alana, and then my father took off for a job
on the oil rigs and never came back.'

'Never?'

'No, never. He didn't stay in touch either. Once
or twice, he sent money to help Mum out but nothing regular and by the time I was four, it stopped
altogether. Mum had a rough time raising us.' Skye
sat down on the hard sofa by the wall while Enzo
crouched down by the fire and fed it more fuel.

'So, what did your mother do?'

'She worked two jobs to get us out of his parents'
house because she didn't feel she should be staying
there, not when my father was sending photos of his
new girlfriend and talking about making a visit.'

'*Dio mio*…where did he think your mother and
his children were going to go?'

'As my grandparents then actually pointed out,
their son wasn't married to Mum and they had both
been kids when they brought me and Alana into the
world. I can see their point too and he was the son
that they loved,' Skye admitted, wanting to be fair
to all parties involved at the time. 'But it was very
hard on Mum because she had no other family to
fall back on.'

'Certainly that must've been a challenge.' Enzo suppressed his outrage on her behalf, recognising that when Skye didn't make a drama out of her difficult childhood, he had even less right. Even so, it went against the grain when he looked back at his own idyllic years of development, cocooned in love and security and appreciation, even his awful little pictures put on display as though they were works of art when he had never had even the smallest ounce of talent in that department. It had never before occurred to Enzo to think of how lucky he had been to have such grandparents, who had given him a decent, loving home.

'Mum got us into an apartment and kept on working and Steve, my stepfather, came along when I was about eight. It took him six years to persuade her to marry him because she didn't trust men, but he was the best thing that ever happened for all of us. He adopted Alana and me and gave us his name. He was the best dad imaginable,' she said sadly, her eyes misting over. 'He was just an ordinary man, a taxi driver, but he was a lovely person.'

'Rather like you...' Enzo reached down to close her tiny hands into his and raised her, wiping the dampness from her cheeks with his thumb. 'I can understand now why your mother started a second family.'

'Brodie and Shona were their world...and they were *so* happy together,' she said chokily.

'I haven't even got that consolation. My parents' marriage was a disaster. My grandparents were frank with me. My father was continually unfaithful, the sort of person who made promises and kept on breaking them. There were several separations and reconciliations. I was conceived during the last of those. I doubt their marriage would have lasted even had they lived,' Enzo stated wryly. 'Did you ever meet your father?'

'No, and it doesn't bother Alana and me,' Skye confessed very quietly. 'Actions speak louder than words and we knew how he treated Mum. Her life would have been so much easier if he had paid support for us but, even though we know that he was earning very well, he never once spared a thought for us and he didn't treat his own parents any better. When they fell ill, it was my mum who helped them out. He was a deadbeat dad, a heartless son and no loss.'

'Sometimes, you're much tougher and less sentimental than I expect.'

'Down to earth,' she corrected with a rueful smile, lilac eyes soft and still a little misty from the tears that had overcome her when she had talked about her stepfather. 'I learned to be, growing up.'

And it made him respect her, Enzo registered in surprise, suddenly aware that he had never respected a woman that way, at least not since his university days when he had learned that he had awarded his love and respect to the wrong woman. Her lies, the calculated treachery enacted by her and his best friend, had wrecked his faith in his fellow humans and he had shut down hard on his emotions, determined never to leave himself that vulnerable ever again.

Skye gazed up, her head tilted back, into Enzo's glittering dark eyes, semi-shielded by his glorious lush black lashes, and her heart was racing and her breath was tripping in her throat. She knew in that moment just how much she had kidded herself when she had believed that she could step back, turn away, *forget* about him. Hardly a realistic possibility of that when she was obsessed with him, when she barely stopped thinking about him even when he was away from her, when in bed at night he was *all* she could think about. And here he was, already so much more interested in her than Ritchie had ever been, already so much more caring.

As he began to step back from her, an almost imperceptible flush accentuating his spectacular cheekbones, she shifted closer. 'Just kiss me,' she urged.

Enzo studied her as if she were insane. 'I can't… you said—'

'What I said a few days ago doesn't matter any more,' she muttered in a rush. 'It doesn't matter that this is only a stupid rebound fling, it's only what we feel that should count.'

'When I tried to tell you that, you wouldn't listen.'

'I'm stubborn and I thought I was doing what I *should* do. Now I know that's not important compared to what I feel,' she told him almost frantically. 'I just want you—'

'And you already know how much I want you, *piccolo mio*,' Enzo groaned, leaning down to her, claiming her parted lips in a passionate assault that sent the very blood rushing through her veins in ecstasy.

He lifted her up against him with gentle hands and her body turned fluid with longing as though he had pressed a button that only he knew how to access. Long fingers trailed up her thigh beneath the skirt of her dress and the ache at the heart of her felt like spontaneous combustion, burning her up from the inside out. Never in her life had she imagined that a man could make her feel like that, but Enzo was teaching her new lessons. Unzipped, her dress fell round her shoulders and he settled her on the side of the bed while he took it off, lifting her up at one point, and every action was so smooth it made her laugh.

'You really are such a womaniser, Enzo.'

'That's not what I want to hear from you.'

'Sorry, I—'

'No, what you think of me isn't crucial, but while I don't deny that there have been a lot of women, I never lied to any of them or cheated on them. I do have standards,' he proclaimed somewhat defensively.

Meeting those unguarded dark eyes of his, Skye

registered in shock that she had hurt him and she paled, shaken that she could have been so tactless, so certain he would be more flattered than offended to be labelled as the paparazzi had categorised him. 'I know you have,' she said softly, hoping to redeem herself.

'Particularly where you're concerned, because if you're about to wake up tomorrow morning and tell me to go cold turkey again, I don't want to do this,' he told her bluntly.

'I promise you I won't do that,' Skye declared unevenly, shaken by that challenge, which she had not been prepared to meet. Yet there was some justification on his part for that cold-turkey comment. She had encouraged him, wanted him, become intimate with him and then slammed the door on their relationship. Of course, Enzo didn't want a relationship, did he? Earlier that day he had reminded her that they were in companion territory, as he had called it then, only that was about to change *again*. Maybe right now his head was spinning a little, as hers was.

'Stop overthinking this, stop worrying,' Enzo urged, crouching down at her feet to flip off her shoes and then the stay-up lace-edged dark stockings that he lingered over with unhidden male appreciation. 'You are such a worrier.'

'How do you know that about me?'

'By watching you. Brodie goes out on his trike round the garden and you hover by the back door like a mother hen even though there's nothing out there that could hurt him. Shona crawls into the hall and you follow her.'

'Possibly I worry too much about keeping them safe.'

'You had good cause but I will not harm you… *ever*,' Enzo swore, ripping off his jacket and embarking on his shirt.

Skye slid off the bed in her lingerie and covered his impatient hands with her own to take over the buttons with a confidence she had never felt in male company before. 'I know that,' she said truthfully, parting the edges of his shirt to splay her fingers across his warm, hard pectoral muscles, heat spearing up inside her, magnifying every sensation. 'I want you so much.'

Oh, no, I didn't say that out loud, she assured herself, but the sudden brilliance of Enzo's dark golden scrutiny warned her that she *had*.

'Feels like months since we were together.'

'It's only been days.' She sighed. 'You're all drama, Enzo.'

'And you're *not*? Banging about the kitchen just because you want me? Treating me like the invisible man?'

Skye reddened at that telling comeback as he tipped her back on the bed, spreading her slender limbs out, narrowed dark eyes glittering with a predator's hunger while he took in her petite curves, cupped in plain white deeply unsexy cotton. 'I love your body,' he confided in a roughened undertone as he removed the rest of his clothing, flung an intimidating handful of condoms on the bedside cabinet and got on the bed to join her.

'Us...we don't make sense.'

'We don't need to make sense,' Enzo told her robustly, strong jawline hard with resolve. 'And I am *not* a rebound fling, stupid or otherwise. I refuse to be a rebound following such a drastic embarrassment as Ritchie the stalker.'

Unexpectedly, Skye found herself grinning, lifting wondering fingers to trace the full line of his soft full lower lip, the pads on her fingers softly tracing through the black shadow of stubble surrounding his sculpted mouth. 'Is that so?'

'I have much more experience than you. You were too naïve to make a major choice like moving in with your first lover.'

'Agreed. Happy now?' Skye asked.

'Won't be happy until I wake up tomorrow and you're still in my arms.'

He detached the light bra, let his lips tease a pink nipple while his fingers moulded her straining flesh and her whole body went haywire with instant response, the tug of his mouth awakening a tightening sensation in her pelvis. Her hips squirmed as his hands ran over her, smoothing, awakening, sending taut little trickles of arousal travelling along her sensitised skin. Fingers sinking into his tousled black hair, she tugged him up to kiss her. And excitement thrummed through her like bolts of white lightning and made her sizzle from head to toe.

'Slow down,' Enzo urged.

'No,' she exclaimed, wrenching at the zip in his trousers, fingers splaying across the hot, hard thrust of him beneath the fine material, her impatience, her need at a level of hunger she had not known she could feel.

'I don't want to hurt you.'

'You're not going to hurt me.'

As long fingers established the slick welcome at the heart of her, Enzo groaned and freed himself in frantic haste from the rest of his clothing. He tipped her back and rose over her with an urgency that finally reflected her own and plunged into her. Sensual shock rippled through her lower body, her inner walls stretching and contracting on his wonderfully effective invasion while little tremors of pleasure gathered and intensified.

'At last,' Enzo framed hoarsely, shifting lithely over her, lean hips circling to settle into a steady rhythm that sent every nerve ending flying and speeded up her heart rate.

Pleasure laced with feverish excitement engulfed her. She moved with him, far more a participant than she had been their first time together, but then she wasn't, she recognised dimly, the same woman she had been even a few weeks earlier. With Enzo, she felt free, equal, safe. As the throbbing beat of desire and need in her pelvis increased, she clung to him, her fingers digging into his shoulders, head thrown back, lips parted and then her climax hit her like a battering ram, throwing her up and tossing her down again with such strength that she cried out and then gasped as the convulsions of delight and satiation followed.

Enzo pulled free of her and flopped back on the bed next to her. *'Dio,'* he husked, out of breath. 'I needed that…and in a few minutes I'm going to need it again.'

Skye laughed, wishing she didn't want him to come back to her and hold her close.

Enzo widened his rich dark golden gaze and looked back at her. *'What?'*

'You're so full of yourself. I bet you were like that in the cradle.' And she stared back at him, heart lurching at the image of a little Enzo throwing his rattle away, expecting it to magically come back and very possibly receiving that amount of attention from a grandmother who, she suspected, from his occasional references, adored him. And why wouldn't she? Enzo had likely exuded that same charisma from a very young age.

He reclined on the bed, naked and unashamed, every inch of his beautiful bronzed body on display. Men weren't supposed to be beautiful, but Lorenzo

Durante was lean, muscular and magnificent, a glorious arrangement of bone and flesh that she found impossible to resist. When had that happened? she wondered. When had her last defences gone down and left her so vulnerable? When she'd tried to walk away in spirit if not in body? It hadn't worked, none of her failsafe plans to protect herself had worked. Enzo had also contrived to draw her in without promises. Nothing she had with him was stable or offered her a future and that terrified her because she already knew that she was falling in love with him and falling deeper and harder than she had ever dreamt possible…and in only a few more weeks, he would probably be returning to Italy.

'What's wrong?'

Skye veiled her eyes, wondering just how Enzo had become so attuned to her every change of mood. 'There's nothing wrong.'

'There had better not be, *piccolo mio*.' Enzo tugged her across the mattress and clamped an arm to her hip. 'We're together now.'

Skye wondered what that meant. How together? As a couple in a relationship? Or as lovers enjoying a brief fling? She reckoned, however, that, bearing in mind Enzo's sensitivities, it was far too soon to be asking for any clarification on that score.

The next morning, Enzo was in a terrific mood and it showed. Although he had as much interest in trees and plants as Skye had in big business, he accompanied Skye and their hosts on the tour of their wintry garden. Throughout that chilly expedition, he kept a hand or an arm anchored to some part of Skye and his attentive display surprised her because she had assumed that in front of his grandparents' friends, he would treat her more casually.

From the castle they travelled straight to the airport and boarded the jet. Skye's mind was untethered, still wandering dizzily through the passionate night they had shared, marvelling at her lack of control and the sheer joy of letting go of her inner critic. Yes, it would hurt when Enzo moved on, as he surely would, but she was strong, she told herself sternly, and she would move on as well when the time came. After all, hadn't she already moved on and past Ritchie?

'Why didn't you tell me about Ritchie turning up at the house yesterday?' she asked Enzo abruptly, marvelling that she had actually forgotten that fact in the excitement of the night that had passed.

He sprang upright, leaning down over her to snap loose her belt, and without the smallest warning he scooped her up out of her seat into his arms.

'Enzo!' she shrieked as he sank down with her still anchored in his arms on the other side of the aisle.

'You were too far away,' he pointed out just as the stewardess appeared, clearly having heard Skye cry out, and her eyes widened at the sight of them together.

Enzo angled his head to smoothly dismiss her again.

Her face hot, her bare feet draped on the arm rest, a muffled giggle escaped Skye as she finally recognised that his shameless spontaneity was one of the things she liked most about him. 'You still haven't answered my question.'

'But you already know the answer.'

Her lilac eyes widened and softened as she looked up at his lean, strong face. He bent his dark head and circled her parted lips with his. Her heart pounded as an electrifying wave of sexual awareness claimed her and she tipped back her head, licking experimentally into his mouth. He responded, sucking her tongue, sending a ripple of sensation through her tautening length. Inner muscles flexed and tightened. She fought to stay in control, embarrassed by the ease with which he overwhelmed her. He ran a long, soothing finger gently down over her cheek.

'You didn't want to bother me,' she said for him.

'You deserved a break from all that. I didn't want you worrying and feeling guilty. Alana was angrier about his visit than she was upset and you must stop blaming yourself for *his* behaviour.'

He claimed her soft, swollen mouth with urgent hunger and she trembled, hopelessly sensitised by the night she had spent in his arms and insanely aware of how much she still wanted him. Slowly he rose and settled her down in the seat opposite him.

'Later,' he murmured with anticipation glittering in his dark golden gaze as the jet powered into landing.

A couple of hours after that, engulfed in the noisy welcome of the children at the house, Skye gathered Shona up and straightened to approach her sister. 'No problems…apart from Ritchie?' she queried.

'I almost forgot. Miss Tomkins, the social worker, called by in the afternoon to check on the kids,' Alana imparted. 'She said she would call in again soon.'

'I wonder how she knew to come here.'

'Apparently, Ritchie gave her the address.'

Skye lost colour, stressed by that information as she wondered what her ex-boyfriend would have said in such circumstances. About her, about the children, about her current living situation. It was an unnerving thought.

CHAPTER EIGHT

'WHY WOULD A social worker be calling on you?' Enzo enquired with a frown.

'I foster Brodie and Shona in a kinship agreement because we're related by blood. Obviously, there's occasional checks to ensure I'm taking proper care of them,' Skye pointed out absently as she helped her sister gather up her coat and bag and saw her to the front door.

When Skye emerged from her sister's hug and closed the front door again, Enzo was still frowning at her. 'I thought you had adopted them?'

'That's the ultimate goal, and I've applied to adopt them, but currently I'm fostering my little brother and sister under the supervision of the social services,' Skye explained ruefully. 'Worst-case scenario, if the authorities are not satisfied by how I'm caring for them, I could lose them.'

'*Lose* them?' Enzo repeated in evident disbelief.

'Yes, my siblings could be taken from me and

placed elsewhere with strangers, even put up for adoption.' Pale and taut at even voicing that frightening possibility, Skye swallowed the sudden thickness in her throat and found her voice again. 'So, naturally I'm worried when I find out that Ritchie directed the social worker here because what else may he have said or insinuated? And I'm already in the wrong for not having immediately contacted the authorities to inform them of our change of address. I intended to but I hung back because I didn't know what best to say about us living here.'

Enzo paced the hall floor, swinging back to shoot her a troubled glance. 'I didn't fully understand your situation. You should have filled me in on these facts sooner.'

'And what difference would that have made? I'll have to admit what happened with Ritchie.' Skye sighed with compressed lips. 'Honesty is always the best policy.'

Skye went through to the kitchen and began to empty the dishwasher. The table and the counters and even the sink were full of dirty dishes. Alana was great with their siblings but not so keen on cleaning up. Skye smiled. She cut her sister a lot of slack on that score because she was aware that Alana dealt daily with some rich, horrendously entitled and arrogant guests in her job at the hotel and was often treated badly in her role.

Enzo retreated to his office to work, flipping open

his laptop. His quick and clever brain was already assessing the likely official response to Ritchie's violence and Skye's current plight. Here she was in temporary employment, intimately involved with her employer and protected everywhere she went by Enzo's security staff because of her unhinged ex-boyfriend. He gritted his teeth and suppressed a groan. None of those facts would look good for her on paper. He knew much more about such official decisions than most people in his age group. A couple of years earlier he had studied his own custody case papers, keen to understand the legal hoops and obstacles his grandparents had traversed to adopt him. When he found it impossible to suppress his concern on the children's behalf and still work effectively, he surrendered and pondered the problem some more before deciding to consult his British lawyer.

Regrettably, that long and frustrating phone conversation told Enzo nothing he wanted to hear. His belief that he could magically sort out Skye's situation died an immediate death when he was very politely informed that his reputation as a notorious playboy would only exacerbate her problems.

'You could only help her by marrying her!' His lawyer chuckled, clearly considering that possibility so far-fetched as to be hilarious. 'Officials involved in care and custody cases look for stable relationships and financial security as a baseline.'

'I'm not thinking of marriage,' Enzo asserted immediately, while his agile intellect pounced on the concept and played with it, turning it round until he could come up with a more acceptable solution. The advantages of such a move piled up even quicker in his brain.

Brodie was in the bath and Skye was towelling dry Shona's hair when Enzo strolled into the bathroom. He had already changed out of his suit into faded jeans and a dark shirt. He rolled up his sleeves, already experienced enough in the bed-and-bath routine to know that Brodie would get him wet.

'I thought you were working. Were we making too much noise?'

'It only gets noisy when I'm here,' Enzo reminded her without embarrassment.

'Enzo,' Brodie proclaimed with a beaming smile and an attitude of deep satisfaction.

'No splashing Enzo,' Skye warned her little brother without much hope because Enzo was as much a fan of splashing games as the toddler.

'No splash,' Brodie promised obediently.

'We'll take them to the zoo on Saturday,' Enzo told her cheerfully.

'It's a very long drive.'

'We'll go by helicopter then.'

Skye heaved a sigh at that careless suggestion but said nothing, striving not to criticise or seem ungrateful for the lifestyle that Enzo enjoyed. For now, they were together, she reasoned, and the children were young enough that they would not remember much about him in a few months' time. She wondered ruefully if she would be able to say the same thing on her own behalf and prayed for a short memory. Right at that moment though, even glancing at Enzo's bronzed profile as he grinned wickedly and capsized one of Brodie's plastic boats, she felt as though she were riding hell for leather for a terribly steep fall. Enzo lit her up like a firework just by being in the same room.

Once the children were fed and in bed, Skye set up the dining room for dinner. She had prepared a casserole for their evening meal, striving to behave as though nothing had changed between her and Enzo when, in truth, everything had changed and she was trying to make little adjustments and avoid making a fuss. A *fuss*? Like asking him where they were going as a couple when obviously they weren't going anywhere, and Enzo's fast-approaching departure would conclude whatever they did have. In short, she was trying to be sensible, not being the woman who hoped against hope for some fairy-tale ending to suddenly pop up in front of her.

'I've had an idea,' Enzo announced over the meal.

Skye pushed her plate away and endeavoured to smother the yawn creeping up on her. Sometimes Enzo's boundless energy was a challenge for her. He strode full tilt into every new day and attacked it like an obstacle course. He didn't slow down as the day progressed. He didn't seem to suffer from her insecurities and if he had worries, he either rose above them or solved them. And even more to the point, the previous night spent in his arms had exhausted her right down to the marrow of her bones.

'You look tired,' Enzo remarked, ebony brows pleating as he scanned the faint purple shadows below her beautiful eyes and the downward curve of her lips.

'I was thinking of an early night...without the usual connotations,' she added in haste as Enzo's dark glittering gaze literally smouldered.

Enzo laughed with considerable amusement. 'As long as you're in my bed.'

'Actually, I was thinking—'

'*My* bed,' Enzo incised without hesitation. 'We don't sleep apart. When I'm back at work I won't see much of you otherwise and we need to make the most of the time we have.'

Disconcerted by that speech and the assurance with which he spoke, Skye felt her cheeks burn even while her heart turned over at the news that he wanted to spend more time with her. 'You said that you'd had an idea?'

'I'm not sure you're ready to hear it yet. When you explained that you were under supervision with the social services, I realised that I had put you in a rather dodgy position. If you were simply working for me, it might be all right, but we're having an affair and some people would view that as a matter of concern, particularly when I'm said to have a… questionable reputation with women,' he framed between compressed lips.

At last he had put a label on what they shared. An affair? It sounded rather racier than Skye felt herself to be, but she couldn't think of any other word to cover their new togetherness. Colour fluctuating, she went off to fetch the coffee. He had seen the same writing on the wall that she had foreseen. Her standing in his life was far from ideal. She was no longer merely a live-in housekeeper, not since they had become much more personally involved. She would look like a foolish, undisciplined woman who had tumbled carelessly out of one disastrous relationship with a man into another that could prove almost as damaging from her siblings' point of view.

Enzo accepted his coffee. 'No comment?'

Skye compressed her lips. 'What you said was true and the children are already attached to you, which is not a good idea when you're leaving.'

'I have a solution to all of it and I would be happy to make the sacrifice.'

'Sacrifice?' Skye interrupted in dismay. 'What on earth are you talking about?'

'You're so good at being a fake girlfriend I think you would be a blast as a fake wife.'

Lilac eyes as wide as they would open stared back at him in disbelief. 'Enzo…are you crazy?'

'I want you to consider the idea. I've become fond of the children and I would pretty much do anything to ensure that you get to keep them with you,' Enzo admitted. 'I consulted my British lawyer for advice—'

'I bet he didn't tell you to marry your penniless housekeeper to help her!' Skye exclaimed, wreathed in mortification as she understood the meaning of that word 'sacrifice' as pertaining to her and the children.

'I'm completely free to marry anyone I want and if I can put you in a better position to adopt your siblings, I'm willing to do it.'

'Well, thank you very much but I'm not willing to accept you as a *sacrifice*!' Skye shot back at him with burning cheeks, thrusting back the dining chair to stand up.

'We have to talk about this.'

'No, we *don't*! We definitely don't!'

'Skye?' Enzo swore under his breath as he watched her pile up dishes to clear the table. 'Sit down and have your coffee.'

She raised a brow. 'Is that an order, sir?'

Enzo dealt her a quelling appraisal. 'It is. But let's take the coffee across the hall and be a little more relaxed.'

'I can't be relaxed when you're talking about marrying me purely to do the kids and me a favour,' she argued.

Ignoring that statement, Enzo swept up the coffee and strode across the hall into the sitting room where she had already lit the corner lamps. He proceeded to seek the controls that would ignite the gas fire because the room was chilly and, while he was still searching, Skye nudged him gently out of the way and took care of it.

'I was planning to start putting up the Christmas decorations tomorrow. Is that all right with you?' she asked brightly, faking it as best she could, keen to change the subject when what he had suggested was sheer insanity.

'You'll have to buy it all new for this place.' Enzo pulled out a credit card and extended it to her as she sank down on the edge of a plush sectional unit. She grasped it with reluctant fingers. 'And stop trying to change the subject.'

'But what you said…about marriage…was ridiculous,' Skye told him tautly. 'You can't say stuff like that.'

'Why not?' Enzo sent her a questioning look, refusing to be either uncomfortable or knocked off topic. 'I'm prepared to deliver on my suggestion. Right now, you need me.'

Skye flipped upright again in frustration and embarrassment. 'I *don't* need you!'

'No?' Enzo stalked closer, dark eyes as hot and golden as the heart of a fire. 'You need me. Without realising what I was doing, I placed you in a difficult position here and then I exacerbated the situation by having sex with you. I wasn't aware that you were in a situation with the children that entailed official scrutiny but I am conscious that my reputation won't do you any favours. Why shouldn't I choose the one option that could sort this mess out?'

'Well, for a start, I can sort out my own problems. You talking nonsense about us getting married is sheer folly!'

Black-lashed eyes of gold shimmered. 'I'm a very good catch,' Enzo quipped with an infuriating grin, lean dark features illuminated by his unholy amusement. 'Well worth the investment of time required and a lot of women would be willing to take the risk on me. I like kids and animals but, most of all, I appreciate very small, slightly built women with curly hair.'

'Enzo…' Skye groaned, her face heating as she recognised herself in that description. 'Stop it.'

'We would only have to stay married until the children are safely and legally yours by adoption. Then we would both take our freedom back and I would ensure that when we separated you, at least, had a decent home for you and your siblings. Once I was gone, you would be able to make a completely fresh start,' Enzo pointed out convincingly.

Once I was gone…

That single phrase reverberated inside Skye like a death knell and ran chills down her spine, making her skin break out in goosebumps. 'It's a very generous offer—' Only not quite the offer that could have thrilled rather than chilled, she recognised guiltily. He meant fake, indeed could only have faced the idea of a marriage that would be a fake. It wouldn't be real, but she would know that from the start. She would also know that it would hurt like hell when she was no longer flavour of the month and he walked away. Her heart sank.

'It's the practical solution to all your worries and it allows us to continue our current arrangement for as long as we choose.'

Skye emitted a second groan. 'Enzo, you wouldn't even be with me if you were living your normal playboy life,' she protested. 'You're only with me now because there isn't much choice in this locality and I'm convenient.'

Enzo reached down to grasp her hand and tugged her upright. '*Madre di Dio*, what did that cowardly little rat do to your self-esteem?' he demanded fiercely. 'Do you truly believe that I suffer from a lack of choice with women? Or that I would simply settle for *convenient*?'

'No, I was trying to explain—'

'I could have called any number of women that I know and invited them to keep me company here. But I met you… I wanted *you…you* in particular, *you especially*,' he emphasised in lethal continuance. 'Absolutely no other woman would have done or could have taken your place.'

His stunning eyes were smouldering gold, luxuriant black lashes low over his intense gaze, his conviction undeniable. Her tummy flipped, her breath catching in her throat, every inch of her pulled taut with tension. 'I shouldn't have said that,' she mumbled, embarrassed now.

'Particularly when it wasn't the truth,' Enzo cut in, one lean hand travelling from her taut shoulder, through the soft, silky fluff of her curls and down to the taut line of her spine. 'You and I are together.'

'In a *relationship*?' she stressed in astonishment.

'We've always been in a relationship,' Enzo countered with unblemished cool, convinced that it was safe to use that word when he was not emotionally invested in it. 'It was never a question of just one night. The moment I had you, I wanted you again and it's still that way.'

'Does that bother you?' she whispered, more seriously this time.

'If you wanted your own bed, it would,' he confided huskily.

As he eased her slight body up against his and he shifted lithely against her, she felt the hard, unashamed promise of his arousal and she trembled, filled to overflowing with sensual awareness. 'So, you're prepared to ask me to marry you on the basis of sex.'

'It's not that basic. Do we really need to go into detail about this attraction?'

Skye stared up at him in silence because that same attraction, that crazy explosive chemical reaction, was tearing her in two. He was talking about marriage and she wasn't stupid, she was intelligent enough to appreciate that a wealthy husband would be an advantage in official terms while a legendary playboy would be a dangerous drawback as a lover, their relationship viewed as insecure and temporary. But Enzo could still offer her and the children a safe future where she could not. As yet, she had neither a permanent home nor reliable employment to offer in her own favour.

And more than anything she yearned for the security of knowing that the young brother and sister she loved to distraction would remain in her care. The fear of losing custody of Brodie and Shona haunted her and made her seriously regret the choice she had made when she had agreed to move in with Ritchie. Of course, Ritchie had talked of marriage as well but there had been no further mention of it once he'd had her within his power.

At least, Enzo was truthful about what he was offering and what he wanted from such an arrangement. A wife who was a wife only on paper. A wife who would agree to a divorce the minute he got bored. He wasn't pretending to love her, he wasn't acting as though he wanted her by his side for ever and wasn't there something to be said about that honesty, wounding as it was? With Enzo, she would know where she stood from the outset, what she could expect from him as well as the terrible truth that a parting was inevitable. The status of a wife was, even so, a lot stronger and safer than that of a casual lover.

'I'll think about it… Have you ever been in love?' she asked weakly.

Enzo grimaced. 'Once was enough. I was young and stupid. I'm not young and stupid any more.'

'Who was she?'

'I don't talk about that. It was years ago!'

'I would still like to know,' she admitted, avoiding his gaze.

'Then you are doomed to disappointment.'

'Did you think of marrying her?'

'Yes, but soon after that I discovered that she had been lying to me and cheating on me. I had a lucky escape.

'Are you thinking about marrying me?' Enzo murmured huskily, the dark timbre of his deep voice making an intimate part of her clench tight with awareness. 'I believe all your worries would be over if you were with me.'

'Of course, I'm thinking about it,' Skye muttered ruefully. 'You're gorgeous and sexy and incredible in bed and I've found you very reliable, in spite of your reputation.'

Enzo stretched out a hand and switched off the fire. 'Leave the cleaning up for the morning. *Incredible?*' he husked.

Skye went red as fire. 'You know you are!'

Enzo closed long fingers round hers to lead her upstairs. Skye pulled free long enough to run around and douse the lights that had been left on.

'You're so responsible,' Enzo told her appreciatively as she joined him on the landing where he awaited her.

'And you don't think about stuff like that because you've never had to worry about bills,' she guessed and then sealed her mouth closed again because sniping at him about his privileged status in life was pointless.

He gathered her into his arms and ravished her parted lips with feverish hunger and then pulled back. 'Sorry, early night *without* interference... I forgot.'

Skye laughed. 'Enzo, you chased my early night right out of my head when you mentioned your idea.'

'You *are* thinking about my suggestion, aren't you?'

'Of course, I am.' But even more, she was wondering about the identity of the woman he had once thought of marrying when he'd deemed himself to be 'young and stupid' and whether that romance had turned him off love and commitment for ever. Evidently the episode still rankled enough that, even now, he didn't want to talk about it.

His room had become their room, although her clothes were still across the corridor in her original room and she wouldn't be moving them any time soon because the wardrobes in Enzo's room were packed to the gills with fancy suits and shirts. Having fetched her cleansing stuff, she removed her make-up while Enzo watched her from the doorway.

'I never saw a woman without make-up until I met you,' he confided.

'And I shouldn't have let you sneak up on me.' Skye pushed him out of the doorway and closed the door in his face while she cleaned her teeth.

'I checked on the kids,' he told her when she reappeared and jumped into bed.

'Some day you'll make a great father,' she whispered as he undressed, although her tummy turned over when she reflected that if she did marry him, she would not be the wife he chose to have a family with. Their marriage would only be temporary.

She tried to close her eyes but the temptation of watching Enzo strip was too great and too strong. Lean, flexing muscle sheathed in golden skin began to emerge and her mouth ran dry and her breathing became audible.

'I feel objectified,' Enzo lamented with dancing dark golden eyes. 'But I love feeling your eyes on me. When are you planning to rip off your clothes for my benefit?'

'That would be…never,' Skye warned him.

Enzo strolled lazily out of the bathroom. 'Never say never around me. Are you thinking about it yet? Has a guy ever received a less enthusiastic response to a marriage proposal?'

'Has ever a woman been told that the prospective bridegroom would be sacrificing himself?'

Enzo vaulted into bed beside her. 'That wasn't diplomatic. It wouldn't be a sacrifice. I have never wanted any woman the way I want you. No matter where you are, what you're doing, what you're wearing.'

'You're just oversexed,' Skye told him, snuggling up to him, one small hand smoothing down over his abs.

'I'm not going to lay a finger on you tonight,' he swore, heavy-lidded dark eyes scanning her face. 'You're tired.'

'Not *that* tired,' Skye teased, allowing that admiring hand to travel south, listening to his groan of startled pleasure with deep satisfaction.

'Possibly I'm off limits until you decide on the proposal.'

'We both know I'm going to say yes because you will keep on and on and on about it until I do.' Skye sighed.

'Now you're talking my language, *piccolo mio*.'

Enzo turned over and pulled her close, running his hands down over her slender back and pulling her slight body over his. 'And we can celebrate.'

'Sacrifices don't celebrate unless they're martyrs.'

Undeterred, he laughed and extracted a long, drugging kiss. A wave of intoxicated happiness washed over Skye. She had said yes to the insanity. But from her point of view, it would be a sensible move as the authorities would much prefer a couple to adopt the children. She would be fine, she told herself urgently, she would live in the moment and look neither forward nor back. Life was too short for regrets and far too colourless without Enzo.

An hour later, just as she was drifting on the edge of sleep, Enzo sprang out of bed, pulled on a pair of jeans and stabbed a number into his phone.

'Who on earth are you calling this late?' she mumbled, watching the unbuttoned jeans slide down to his hip bones, leaving her to look at a flat hard stomach traversed by a dark furrow of hair.

'Chiara, a friend of mine, and it's not too late an hour for a party girl and the best wedding planner in Italy,' he explained, switching to liquid Italian and settling into a very long and animated conversation while Skye slowly wakened, galvanised into the act by those magic words, 'wedding planner'.

'Wedding planner?' she queried as he set his phone aside with an air of satisfaction.

'Yes, she'll fly over here tomorrow. We're thinking the Maldives. We could do with a bit of sunshine.'

'The *Maldives*?' she exclaimed.

'It's the right time of year and then we'll be home here for Christmas.'

'Enzo, I would need permission from the authorities to take the children out of the country!'

'Then get it organised. Set up a meeting for us, whatever…' Enzo spread an eloquent brown hand to underscore his urgency. 'We have to get this show on the road and there's some stuff I can't do for you. I'll ring my grandparents and tell them what's happening at breakfast time. You should put Alana on alert. I assume you want her at the wedding? And we ought to consider a nanny for the occasion as well.'

Now fully awake as that detailed list of instructions penetrated, Skye sat up in bed and stared back at him, her eyes huge. He was overflowing with raw energy, dark eyes glittering, vitality and impatience splintering from every inch of his long, lean body. 'It's one in the morning, Enzo. What on earth are you planning to tell your grandparents about us?'

'The truth, only the truth. It wouldn't be fair to let them believe that we were a real for-ever couple, but that won't stop them dreaming the dream and hoping we fall for each other regardless of what I've said.' Enzo frowned. 'They'll be disappointed but there's not much I can do about that.'

Skye tried and failed to come up with a conversational response. He had silenced her. 'We could get married here,' she pointed out weakly.

'Not very festive. It's dull and damp and wet. I like sunshine.'

Skye nodded slowly. 'I'll contact our case worker when the office opens.'

'My legal team will take care of any legalities involved.'

'So, it seems we are definitely getting married,' she commented shakily.

'And all you need to worry about is what you wear,' Enzo asserted with satisfaction.

He would make her happy, he reasoned. He would stay married to her until she had her life and her future plans sorted out. He reckoned that that would take at least a year to achieve. A year was no time at all. It would be a practical arrangement that met both their needs. And he needed her, he needed her very much at present, although he was certain that that driving need to be with her would fade as time moved on.

CHAPTER NINE

'I LIKE THE tree and the traditional colours,' Enzo declared from the kitchen doorway a week later as Brodie whooped at his arrival and Shona began to fast-crawl towards him.

Skye gazed back at him for a split second, drinking him in like a dangerous drug. His tie was loose at his throat, stubble roughening his bronzed skin in denial of that sleek sophisticated elegance that was the norm for him. Instead, he simply looked all male and dangerously, smoulderingly sexy, particularly when he watched her through narrowed dark eyes framed with lashes so dense they doubled as eyeliner. Something clenched low in her tummy and she struggled to put her thoughts together again.

'Dinner's almost ready. Alana was here all afternoon and she helped me with the Christmas decorations. Keeping Shona away from the tree is a challenge but I put some soft things on the low branches, so that even if she pulls them, she can't do much damage,' Skye explained. 'We've got another meeting with the case worker tomorrow. There are forms to fill in and they want to meet you again. That's at ten. Can you make it?'

'Yes.' As she reached out to open the oven and check on dinner, Enzo stepped between her and the door and lightly grasped her wrist to deftly ease a ring onto her wedding finger.

Skye froze in surprise.

'An engagement ring? I wasn't expecting *that*,' she confessed with a frown of discomfiture, holding her hand up so that the light from the window illuminated the large oval stone that glittered and sent rainbow facets dancing across the tiled floor. 'A sapphire?'

'It's a very rare blue diamond,' Enzo told her casually. 'But don't get excited about it. It's only window dressing.'

In receipt of that statement, the thrill factor dropped to zero for Skye, although she still could not help staring fixedly at the ring because the jewel was magnificent. Enzo had deliberately chosen to give her the ring in the kitchen and without ceremony, bluntly emphasising how far removed both the ring and their relationship were from real romance. 'It's beautiful. I won't say thanks because I won't be keeping it but I'm sure I'll enjoy wearing it.'

'An update on the wedding plans,' Enzo continued. 'My legal team tells me that a marriage in the

Maldives wouldn't be lawful, and my grandmother tells me that if I don't get married in my childhood church she will be heartbroken. Therefore, we will get married in Italy, have the reception there and then fly on to the Maldives for a couple of nights.'

'Yes, your grandmother has already phoned me to explain.' Skye was amused to see that Enzo was disconcerted by that news. 'Apparently your PA had my phone number and she passed it on. I spoke to your grandmother this afternoon. She may have forgotten to ask my shoe size but she got everything else there is to know about me in triplicate.'

'Nonna doesn't miss a trick,' Enzo quipped. 'I'm sorry.'

'No, no need to apologise. Your family don't know me and all of a sudden, you're marrying me. Your grandmother was warm, friendly and delightful. I have no complaints.'

'They wanted to fly over and meet you and the children before the wedding even though they're aware that the wedding is more a paper event than a real one,' he confided. 'I told them that we'd be too busy getting all our ducks in a row in time for the wedding and requesting permission for the children to accompany us. You'll have to go shopping and you'll need swimwear et cetera for the Maldives, as well as all the bridal stuff.'

'I don't even know where to start.'

'Chiara will make arrangements for the bridal end of things. She's a seasoned operator.'

'And a friend, you said?'

'I've known her since I was a teenager.'

They had eaten and Skye had got the children to bed when the doorbell sounded.

'It's Chiara… Paola texted me that she had arrived. She's staying at the Blackthorn Hotel. She asked if she could stay here but we need our privacy. Of course, she'll be curious about you.'

'I suppose,' Skye conceded nervously on her path to the front door, turning her head, her voice dropping as she glanced back at Enzo with a troubled expression. 'Before we go any further, you *are* sure about marrying me, aren't you?'

'Nobody ever made me do anything I didn't want to do…aside from my grandfather. Stop worrying,' he urged.

The sleek sports car parked outside and the woman on the doorstep were not at all what Skye had expected. Chiara was almost six feet tall and towered over her. She was built like a leggy supermodel with long blonde hair halfway to her waist and a perfect face. She was also clad head to toe in skin-tight midnight-blue leather leggings and a fitted jacket. Breezing past Skye without even looking at her, she headed straight for Enzo and a flood of Italian broke from her in a wave.

'Use your English, Chiara. Come and meet Skye.' Enzo closed his hand to Skye's to bring her forward and introduce her. 'Skye is your client and the bride-to-be.'

Chiara surveyed Skye in literal wonderment, much as though a worn hall rug had stood up and tried to trip her. 'Skye...how lovely to meet you. I hope you're free for the next forty-eight hours at least. I need to know your taste in *everything* before we can get organised.'

Enzo smiled at both women. 'I'll be working.'

Skye showed the blonde into the sitting room and offered her refreshments.

'I'd prefer a drink to coffee,' Chiara told her.

'I'll open one of Enzo's bottles of wine.'

When Skye returned with a glass of wine for both of them, the blonde opened a sleek tablet and proceeded to ask for preferences in colours and styles. 'It's a shame Enzo's grandparents are so determined to get heavily involved. It'll have to be a modest traditional dress to please them, which cuts your options down.'

'I suspect that I'll choose something fairly traditional anyway.'

Chiara was very efficient but she shot in loads of personal questions, which Skye carefully sidestepped, assuming that the information that their marriage would be a paper sham had been disclosed only to Enzo's grandparents.

'It sounds like it was love at first sight,' Chiara re-marked after Skye had admitted meeting Enzo by the side of the road, although Skye had not mentioned that she had been fleeing an assault by her former boyfriend. 'That doesn't fit Enzo's profile. He pre-fers a challenge, and you being here and available on site—'

'Is just what I enjoy most,' Enzo chipped in from the doorway.

Chiara raised a brow. 'If you say so, but, let me tell you, none of your friends are likely to believe this caper is for real.'

'I think, if that is your attitude,' Skye interposed tautly, 'you should leave me to organise our wed-ding.'

'Perfectly said, *piccolo mio*.' Enzo studied the blonde, who had flushed. 'I know you can be nice if you want to be nice, Chiara. What's it to be?'

'I will mind my own business and say nothing more,' Chiara responded tightly. 'I *want* to do this wedding. It will be the society event of the year and I want it on my résumé to impress my other clients.'

Amused by that candour, Skye stood up to fetch another glass and poured wine for Enzo.

'You look after him. *Dio mio*, no wonder he's in seventh heaven!' Chiara exclaimed. 'Enzo, if that secret had got out sooner, you'd have had a queue of happy housewives at your door years ago.'

Ironically, Skye had some sympathy for that tart

aside. Enzo *did* enjoy being looked after and she didn't mind doing it because he was always appreciative and he didn't take advantage. Clearly, Chiara had never wished to take care of any man but then every relationship was different and what was right for her might not be right for someone else.

'Skye is not a housewife. She's a teacher.'

'But surely you won't be working?'

'We'll have to see,' Skye said equably, knowing very well that in the not so distant future she would be looking for another teaching position, keeping up her own life and independence to lay the basis for the time when she would be living alone again.

Chiara sighed like someone in pain when she saw the engagement ring and raved about it. By the time she departed, Skye was heartily bored with discussing wedding finery but she was looking forward to seeing the gowns that were to be brought to the house for her.

'Chiara has an acid tongue,' she remarked thoughtfully once they were alone again.

'Her parents went through a very nasty divorce when she was a teenager, and she developed that edge afterwards.'

'She's kind of possessive of you,' Skye continued doggedly. 'Did you date her at one stage?'

'No, but I slept with her when I was fifteen. She was my first. It was casual, friendly, nothing either of us viewed as important at the time.'

'I knew it.' Skye groaned. 'It was the way she looked at you. I didn't like it, but I can ignore it. Your grandmother did say she's very good at her job.'

'I love your practicality,' Enzo confided, tucking her face into his chest, where she drowsily breathed in the scent of him like an unrepentant addict as they climbed the stairs.

Skye pulled her head back. 'I have to go to court tomorrow afternoon for the non-molestation order to be granted against Ritchie.'

'I know. Your solicitor advised me. I'll accompany you.'

'No, I don't want that. You shouldn't get involved,' Skye told him anxiously. 'Ritchie will be there as well and I don't want you associated with me for his benefit. He's dangerous.'

'Associated? We're getting married!' Enzo countered squarely.

'Stay out of it. It's my mess and I will deal with the consequences. Imagine what the press could do with it if you were recognised and we'd both be embarrassed if his attack on me came out in public.'

Enzo frowned. 'You'll have a protection team with you tomorrow.'

'Of course.'

Enzo compressed his lips. 'I'd prefer to be there in person to support you.'

'I know you would, but some things are mine to handle.'

* * *

In the midst of the very busy two weeks that followed the children came down with chickenpox and Skye ended up sleeping in their room every night to be within easy reach when they woke up crying from feverish dreams and needing soothing. The non-molestation order was granted and Ritchie was no longer allowed to contact or approach Skye.

That had been a relief but the sight of Ritchie, bitter, flat-eyed and threatening in the courtroom, had unnerved her. She marvelled that she had ever believed he loved her or that she had loved him. His expressions in court had shown his nastiness and she shuddered, thinking of how close he had come to killing her. No matter how hard she had stood tall on the outside, on the inside she had still felt sick and scared at being that close to him again.

The night before their Italian wedding and within hours of their flight to Italy, however, disaster struck. Enzo's mobile rang while they were eating and he sprang out of his chair, his voice rising in volume as he demanded repetition and clarification. Pocketing his phone, his face stamped with tension and urgency, he strode to the door.

'What's happened?' Skye jumped up out of her seat, registering that there was some sort of crisis afoot.

'The factory's on fire!' Enzo bit out rawly. 'The

security guard has been taken to hospital. Someone knocked him out.'

'Good heavens…what do you want me to do?' It was almost their wedding day, she thought in dismay.

'It's doubtful that I'll be able to fly out with you now. I'll join you as soon as I can. Don't worry… I'll make it,' Enzo promised grittily.

Skye swallowed a groan and raced out to the hall after him. 'Enzo!'

If the factory had gone up in flames, it would be very hard for him to leave the UK. 'Maybe we should postpone the wedding,' she suggested reluctantly as he swung back from the front door.

Enzo angled his tousled dark head back to her, his dark eyes unusually grave. 'No way, not when we've finally got everything ready to go.'

Skye couldn't sleep and got up early, creeping around, keen to avoid waking up the children. She reckoned she would be flying out to Italy alone without Enzo and meeting his grandparents without him present to ease the introduction. At the same time though, she would have Alana, Isabel, the bright and cheery young nanny Enzo had hired, and Shona and Brodie with her. She would manage, she told herself, she always did.

The afternoon of that same day in the privacy of the bedroom set aside for her to dress in his grandparents' home, Skye recalled that brief exchange and wondered what would happen if Enzo didn't arrive in Italy on time, because he was cutting it fine. What if he jilted her at the altar? Her tummy gave a sick lurch. No, Enzo would never leave it to the very last moment, nor would he ever seek to humiliate her.

As the owner of the packaging business, Eduardo Martelli, Enzo's grandfather, had been in constant touch with the authorities and Enzo. Skye was already aware that arson was suspected. The fire was out but a great deal of damage had been done and the professionals were currently trying to decide whether a total rebuild of the factory or a restoration and an extension to the building would work the best.

Alana, vibrant in an emerald-green bridesmaid dress, literally burst through the door. 'Enzo's arrived! He wanted to come up and see you but his grandmother won't allow it because she says it's bad luck for the groom to see the bride before the church!' she gabbled and then she stopped to stare at her older sister. 'My goodness, Skye…you look magical in that gown.'

Enzo was finally, safely under the same roof. Much of Skye's anxiety drained away and a smile stole the tension from her generous mouth. She studied her reflection in the wardrobe mirror. Her dress was made of lace that sparkled when the crystal beads caught the light. It had long tight sleeves, a fitted bodice, a sweetheart neckline and a narrow skirt. Chiara had complained that it was dull but Skye didn't like frills or too much embellishment.

There was only a very small removable train and her veil was short and attached to the beautiful pearl tiara that Sophie Martelli had insisted on loaning her. The beauty of the gown lay in the exquisite lace from which it was fashioned and its classic design.

As she descended the imposing staircase with Alana at her heels, she passed by a framed photograph of Enzo as a teenager, an Enzo who, by the wicked sparkle in his eyes, was often up to no good. Enzo had never been an angel, she reckoned, but he had a surprisingly serious side to his nature. He had been devastated by the fire at Mackies, particularly when everything had been going so well there and now business was at a standstill. He intended to stay longer in the UK to supervise the rebuild. Once he committed to something, he stayed committed.

He had grown up in an old, gracious family house where he had been very much loved. Yet somewhere along the line his faith in other people had sunk without trace, filling him with restlessness and distrust. Had that change been caused by that long ago relationship that had gone wrong for him at university? Or was it simply the influence of the Durante wealth that he had not been allowed to escape? Sophie, who had asked Skye to call her Nonna, had shown her photo albums. Enzo was the very image of his late father, whose life had stumbled from one disaster to the next, and his grandparents had done everything within their power to ensure that Enzo enjoyed a different outcome.

He had come to *her* rescue, Skye conceded as she climbed with care into the beribboned wedding car with her sister and Eduardo Martelli, who, in the absence of any male relative on her side, had offered to walk her down the aisle. Enzo had so many positives going for him. He had been marvellous with her and the children, in spite of the fact that he was not a domesticated male, eager to settle down with one woman.

Enzo desired her but what was that worth at the end of the day when there was nothing surer than the fact that eventually another woman would come along whom he desired even more? Their marriage had an agreed end date and she needed to keep that in mind. She had signed a prenup, packed with cold, hard financial facts. She knew the score. She shouldn't be continually thinking about Enzo, missing him or worrying about him. She had got in too deep, far too deep, she scolded herself, her fingers tightening round her bouquet.

'You're nervous. I wasn't expecting that,' Alana confided as they entered the big church in the village.

At first glance Skye felt as though she were standing in a field of flowers because every surface seemed to be decorated with beautiful blooms and ribbons and the candles were lit, illuminating the man at the altar. Enzo wore a dove-grey morn-

ing suit and he stood there, tall and strong and incredibly masculine from his broad shoulders to his
long, powerful legs. He didn't look remotely nervous, he looked cool as ice and confident, possibly
even a little impatient for the ceremony to begin,
and she smiled because that complete innate assurance was so Enzo.

There was something incredibly appealing about
Skye's smile, Enzo reflected calmly. He could see
how nervous she was and it tightened something in
his chest. The small quick wedding he had envisaged
had turned into a massive elaborate event to which
everyone who was anyone was invited, both the elite
of society and the business world. The church was
packed and his bride had done him proud. She was
the picture of elegance, her slender delicacy encased
in lace that somehow sparkled, just as her personality did. His grandparents loved her and the children,
had already mentioned how much natural class she
had and how admirable was her devotion and loyalty
to her siblings. She was a hell of a girl and, for the
first time, he found himself acknowledging that it
was a great shame that their marriage would be fake.

That very thought shook him inside out and he
paled, hands clenching into fists. So, he had grown
fond of her and the children, even the stupid dog,
well, that was no crime and hardly surprising in the
circumstances, he told himself. He strove to ignore

Shona, sitting on his grandmother's lap and stretching out hopeful arms to him while Brodie sulked on Isabel, the nanny's knee, having already made a break for freedom several times and been thwarted. He knew they would be lucky to get through the ceremony without the toddler throwing a tantrum.

He had got attached to them all and when they split up, he would keep on visiting them. At least until Skye met someone else. His teeth gritted fiercely at that idea, but he knew that she was far too lovely to be left on any shelf as a single parent. She was beautiful, intelligent and unfailingly loyal and honest. She would be a major catch for any man, just not him.

As they knelt before the priest, Skye noticed that Enzo seemed to have become very tense and she linked her fingers with his and squeezed and he sent her a gleaming glance of amusement. The elderly priest talked while Enzo quietly translated the gist of the ceremony. Before she knew where she was, Enzo was sliding the ring onto her finger and snatching her close for a kiss.

'Enzo!' she scolded and saw his grandmother laughing.

And then her lips shifted beneath the soft firmness of his and she quivered, heat sparking at the heart of her and stirring an ache that reminded her of just how long it had been since they had made love. The chickenpox had been as effective as a vote of celibacy and had kept her firmly clamped to the children and by the time they had recovered, she had been exhausted and stressed out and Enzo had told her to catch up on her beauty sleep.

A blaze of cameras awaited them outside the church and it was a relief to escape into the limousine and be ferried off to the hotel where the reception would take place. 'I didn't realise there would be so many guests,' she confided.

'There will be many more joining us at the hotel. The church wasn't big enough to take everyone. I suspect children I played with in kindergarten may even have been included. Nonna wanted everyone I ever knew to have the opportunity to attend.'

Skye blinked, wondering if his former love from university had been included and asking before she could think better of the question.

Enzo slung her a stunned appraisal. 'Of course not! Why would she be invited?'

Skye ignored the anger flaring in his dark golden eyes. 'So, you didn't stay friends,' she gathered.

'Why are you so curious?' he demanded impatiently.

Skye widened her eyes. 'You tell me that you've only been in love once in your life and you expect me *not* to be curious?'

Enzo shrugged a broad shoulder. 'I don't discuss it.'

'Even though you know every good, bad and ugly

thing there is to know about me?' Skye questioned, lilac eyes bright with challenge. 'And what's more, *expect* to know it?'

'Even though,' he confirmed, determined to close the topic.

Total silence fell.

'I didn't even get to tell you how gorgeous you look in that dress.'

'And that compliment is not exactly falling on fertile ground now,' Skye pointed out without apology.

They arrived at the hotel to be engulfed by a flood of guests. The introductions seemed to go on for ever. Skye's mouth ached from smiling and she flexed fingers stiff from handshakes. The instant she was free from the line-up she went off to reunite with her smallest siblings. Shona sat in her arms saying, 'Zozo? Want Zozo.'

'Enzo... *Enzo*,' Brodie sounded out importantly for his little sister's benefit.

'I suppose we've had our first row,' Skye remarked when she took her seat by his side at the bridal table.

'Merely a difference of opinion,' Enzo contradicted.

'The next time you want to know something about me, I'll do a brick-wall shutdown on you.' While Skye knew that their sexual chemistry was amazing, Enzo's ongoing refusal to confide in her merely emphasised the fact that their marriage wasn't a real one, she conceded ruefully.

An unexpected chuckle fell from Enzo's lips. 'I will give you a hint. The stories I refuse to tell you are the ones that make me feel like a fool.'

'Like the dinner-party disaster,' Skye guessed, in more charity with him after that admission.

'My grandparents and Alana have offered to look after the kids while we're in the Maldives,' Enzo imparted. 'Nonna pointed out that a twelve-hour flight for such young children wasn't the best idea and we are only going to be there for forty-eight hours.'

'I thought Alana was coming with us.'

'She told me that she doesn't much fancy being a third in a party for two. We'll be spending our wedding night on the jet. I'd prefer to take Brodie and Shona away when we have more time to spend with them.'

It was a sensible suggestion and Skye simply ensured that she enjoyed time with the children that afternoon, freeing Alana up to chat to other guests and dance. It was wonderful to see her sister relax and have a good time for a change. Alana had changed so much after the death of their parents, focusing only on work and how much she could earn, where once she had been focused purely on art and money hadn't seemed to matter to her. Now she worked endless overtime in a menial job. Their sudden responsibility for their younger brother and sister had forced them both to grow up faster than was comfortable and much of the fun had gone out of their lives, Skye acknowledged ruefully.

It was a lively celebration, powered by catchy music, dancing and laughter. Italians, Enzo told her with pride, knew how to party. Skye's throat ached with talking and she had to dig deep for the energy to stay on the dance floor and keep up with Enzo. When it was time to leave, she went upstairs with her sister to remove her wedding dress and change into a comfortable outfit in which to travel.

'That was a very long day and you are very tired,' Enzo commented in the limo on the way to the airport as she flopped back in the corner.

'But it's our wedding night.' As soon as she said it, her cheeks burned an almost painful red because once again she felt as though she was parading too many feelings that he did not share. It was a sham marriage and they were lovers but not in the romantic everlasting sense. Enzo could live without her. Enzo *would* move on to other women. The promises they had exchanged at the altar were meaningless.

'All you'll be doing on the flight is sleeping. You're dead on your feet,' Enzo said drily. 'Tomorrow we'll wake up to sunshine and blue skies.'

'Yes,' she conceded sleepily, smiling.

He took her hand as they walked into the airport flanked by his security team. 'Her name was

Allegra—the name of the woman I loved,' he told her in a driven undertone.

'Tell me about her…if you want?' Skye tacked on that last qualifier on a questioning note at his unexpected willingness to talk.

'I don't want to, but I shouldn't have secrets from you,' Enzo conceded tautly as they boarded the jet. 'You have kept none from me.'

Warmed by that belated concession, Skye sank down into a seat in the opulent cabin.

'Allegra's cousin, Niccolò, was my best friend at university. We were both equally into sport and I met Allegra through him. They were cousins who grew up together in close families. Their fathers were twin brothers who'd married sisters and they all lived in the same town. They even looked like siblings.'

'What was she like?' Skye interrupted, surprised that he was choosing to tell her so much about his former girlfriend's background.

'A vivacious brunette who loved to dance, the life and soul of every party. I fell for her very quickly and I was with her over two years before I asked her to marry me. We planned to marry after our graduation.'

'What went wrong?' Skye asked when he fell silent.

'I went home for the weekend to tell my grandparents. I got a mixed reaction. Nonno had no objections, but my grandmother thought Allegra was what she termed *secretive* and that I shouldn't rush into setting a date. That night I drove over to the apartment Allegra shared with her cousin and as I was parking my car, I saw a silhouette behind the blinds of a couple kissing. They often had friends in, so I thought nothing of it,' he admitted.

A sinking suspicion infiltrated Skye and she stiffened in dismay.

'They weren't expecting me. They had no guests either. I just looked at them together…and I *knew* but I couldn't understand *why* they were pretending that their relationship was only familial. Everything else fitted in. Allegra had refused to move in with me, insisting that her parents wouldn't like it. Although I spent the night with her there occasionally, she never gave me a key. Behind closed doors they were free to do as they liked.'

'What did you do?' Skye whispered sickly.

'I confronted them. Ironically it was Niccolò who came clean first. I think he'd been so jealous, he almost enjoyed telling me. Allegra, however, lied to the bitter end. Apparently, they fell for each other as teenagers and their families were horrified. Although being with a cousin is not illegal, their parents believed that they were too genetically close to ever be a couple, so their relationship went underground but it never stopped. They had continued having sex the whole time I was with her. That turned my stomach,' Enzo admitted with a grimace.

'I'm not surprised,' Skye commented, feeling a little queasy too at the extent of the deception that had been practised on him.

'I was shattered. I had fallen in love with a girl who didn't exist. She had picked me out and told him to become my friend. She needed a boyfriend to keep her family in the dark. Being with me and Niccolò being my friend gave them endless excuses to be together without rousing any suspicions. She was planning to go the whole way and marry me. I doubt if any children we might have had would have been mine.'

'What happened next?'

'I never spoke to either of them again. I didn't tell anyone what had happened. I felt like such a stupid, gullible idiot for not suspecting them sooner,' he bit out ruefully. 'I told my grandparents that I had caught her cheating on me. The rest of it was too sordid for their ears. Allegra and Niccolò set out to use me and succeeded for over two years. I've never forgotten that.'

Skye could only begin to imagine how humiliated Enzo must have felt once he knew the truth. They had lied to him and deceived him without shame in a calculated betrayal of trust. 'Nothing that they did to you was excusable. They should've stood up to their families and gone for testing to see if there was any medical reason why they couldn't be together.'

'Agreed, but Allegra is why I don't do love,' Enzo

confided as he buckled in and the jet engines fired up. 'It blinds you, makes you vulnerable. You can have a very good time with a woman without handing over your soul.'

'I'm so sorry that happened to you,' Skye told him and as soon as a light meal had been served, she fell into the bed in the sleeping compartment like a rock dropped from a height.

Skye woke the following morning to dappled sunlight playing across an unfamiliar wooden ceiling, rays and shadows playing over the muslin drapes on the bed and screening the windows. She had a guilty recollection of being roused by Enzo to leave the plane, then stumbling through a busy airport and into transport. She remembered him helping her to undress and sliding into bed and she now felt wonderfully rested for the first time in weeks. There was a dent in the pillow beside hers, telling her that Enzo had slept beside her.

She showered and dug into her case for a bright red bikini. Tugging back the screen doors, she walked out onto the wooden pier outside. The sea, almost as clear as glass, rippled only inches beneath her. She could see pebbles, tiny colourful fish and shells and above her the sky was a deep strong cobalt blue. The sunshine poured down on her and she lifted her face dreamily into that golden heat, soaking up the warmth on her skin.

'Morning, sleepyhead. I ordered breakfast for us when I heard you in the shower,' Enzo murmured, and she jerked round to focus on him.

Clad only in a pair of swim shorts, he stood by one of the pier struts, his long, lean, bronzed length gleaming wetly. He had clearly just climbed out of the water and every single strong line of his powerful body, from his wide shoulders to his hard abdomen and narrow waist, was delineated in the sunshine. She watched a water bead slowly trickle down over his muscular torso. Her nipples pinched taut inside her bra and her tummy clenched. As always, he looked magnificent. Clothed or unclothed, Enzo was gorgeous. And she was married to him now. No, don't get carried away with that knowledge, she scolded herself. Remember it's not real, it's just a short-term marriage.

'I don't remember seeing a resort last night, but then I don't remember much of anything.' She sighed with a guilty wince.

'The resort is out of view to the right at the end of the pier. This island we're on is totally private,' he told her. 'Only the staff have access. I'm looking forward to skinny dipping at midnight.'

'Breakfast is on its way,' she noted, strolling down to the table set in the shade, glancing across at the island, which was covered with lush palm trees running down to a white sand beach. 'This is idyllic. My apologies for sleeping like Rip van Winkle.'

An appetite-tempting array was delivered to the table. 'Gosh, I'm starving!' Skye confided, reaching for a piece of tropical fruit and then a pancake. 'I was too stressed to eat much yesterday.'

Coffee and tea were poured. Enzo stretched back in his chair, dark golden eyes locked to her as he ate a croissant. 'Sleepy or not, I still fancy the pants off you, Signora Durante. And I'm appreciating the downtime here. We needed a break.'

Eating her fruit, she rested back feeling gloriously relaxed. 'Any news about the fire?'

His lean, darkly handsome features tensed. 'The arson has been confirmed. An accelerant was used and they have the evidence. The stores went up like a bonfire and spread to the factory. The security man saw nothing. Someone came at him from behind. The surveillance cameras may show something but one of them was offline.'

He discussed his plans for the rebuild, confessed that the architect had already sent him some rough sketches and then he laughed. 'I got up at six and touched base with everyone. Twelve months ago, I never saw the dawn. I was partying half the night but I was incredibly bored. I much prefer work to boredom and I like a routine. I will hate admitting it to my grandfather but blackmail works on me.'

Her smooth brow indented. *Blackmail?*

Without fanfare, Enzo explained the agreement he had made with the older man following what he referred to as 'the dinner-party episode'. 'And the irony is that I'm much happier working than when I was chasing the next big thrill.'

'I can't comment because I didn't know you before.'

'You wouldn't have liked me. I was a case of arrested development. I think I've finally finished growing up.'

'You still haven't told me about the dinner-party thing,' she reminded him, amusement dancing in her bright eyes.

Enzo grimaced. 'My companion got under the table and tried to unzip me.'

'No?' Skye framed in disbelief.

Enzo winced. 'In the middle of the meal because she was bored stiff. I then had an embarrassing struggle with her to get her back into her seat, but it was more my fault than hers. Neither of us were sober and she had no idea how to behave in company.'

Skye groaned. 'What were you thinking of?'

Enzo sprang upright, stalked round the table and bent down to scoop her bodily out of her seat. 'I think much more efficiently around you,' he told her as she laughed. 'And I have learned to appreciate common sense.'

'Common sense isn't sexy.' Skye wrinkled her nose.

'It is when you see the opposite in action. And you

come out here in a minuscule scarlet bikini and say you're *not* sexy?' Thrusting open the screen doors, Enzo tumbled her down on the bed.

'It's not minuscule. It's just that I don't have a lot to put in it,' she lamented.

'More than enough for me.' Enzo crushed her lush mouth hungrily beneath his and groaned, stretching over her slight body and sliding between her legs. 'And now I've got to wrestle you out of the blasted thing.'

Skye rolled away and sat up with a giggle. She tugged off the top and the bottoms with alacrity while he watched her with answering amusement.

'You missed me,' he commented with satisfaction.

'Of course, I did,' she muttered, recalling all those lonely nights of broken sleep in the children's room.

Enzo spread an appreciative hand over a small pouting breast and bent his head to capture the rosy nipple in his mouth. 'Never stop being that honest with me,' he urged.

'Why would I?' she framed, thoughts blurring as the tug of his lips sent an urgent shot of pure, naked craving down into her pelvis.

He kissed a haphazard line down over her body, found the heart of her and dallied there, long fingers toying with her tender entrance while he tormented her with his mouth and the tip of his tongue. She hit a peak so fast it left her breathless and, with an audible hiss of enthusiasm, he flipped her over, lifted her and drove into her from behind, punctuating that move with a revealing groan of deep satisfaction.

Excitement gripped her from head to toe because she was so sensitive, his every thrust set her on fire. She couldn't get enough of him. He couldn't get enough of her. Perspiration filmed her skin and she careened into another breathtaking climax with the sound of his name on her lips. She collapsed on the bed and Enzo pulled her close.

'I like you screaming my name,' he said raggedly.

'I didn't scream!'

'You said my name with wonderful enthusiasm. I liked it,' Enzo rephrased smoothly, sitting up to lift her over him and wrapping both arms round her.

'I feel like a cuddly toy.' Skye pressed her lips against a bare brown shoulder, still intoxicated by the delicious sensations thrumming through her limp body.

'I'm working up to carrying you into the shower and then we'll explore the island and go waterskiing.'

'What if I don't like it?'

'We'll try something else. I'm very flexible.'

Two days passed in a whirl of activity. Skye preferred jet-skiing to waterskiing because she couldn't stay upright for long on the water. They went snorkelling and sailing in a catamaran. They also dined on the beach and went skinny dipping afterwards, sitting long into the night on the shore with drinks. Enzo gave her a beautiful gold watch and Skye

picked a souvenir bauble for the Christmas tree back
home. He confessed that he was missing Brodie and
Shona, which touched her heart, and he bought a pile
of toys for them.

They slept on the flight, Enzo up early, back in
a sleek, sophisticated business suit. They had had
so much fun, she reflected as she pulled on jeans
and a sweater, prepared for the icy temperatures that
awaited her back home. She had to pick Brodie up
from his playgroup. She still felt dizzy with happiness after forty-eight hours of Enzo. She didn't feel
that she should be so happy but Enzo was in excellent form as well.

Oh, who are you trying to kid? she asked herself in exasperation as she put on her ankle boots.
Even though she had kept warning herself to keep
her head in Enzo's vicinity because their marriage
wasn't destined to last, she had still fallen for Enzo
like a ton of bricks. How could she not have fallen
for him? From the outset he had looked out for her
in every way possible. He had cared for her, sup-
ported her and never once put her down. He made
her feel special and he shared everything with her.
Of course, she had fallen madly in love with him,
but she wasn't planning to tell him and she wasn't
going to make a fuss about it either.

Some day in the future, Enzo would announce
that he was returning to Italy and she would have to
deal with it. She wouldn't throw her feelings in his

face. He didn't deserve that when he had been honest with her from the beginning. It wasn't a proper marriage. Enzo had never planned to stay with her and the children, she reminded herself. He would leave and she would have to make the best of the situation.

They parted at the airport. 'I'm catching a lift with my security team to the factory,' Enzo explained. 'I'll try not to be late tonight. I want to see the kids.'

When Skye got back to the house, eager to see Alana and Shona, she was disappointed. Alana had left a note explaining that she had taken Shona out shopping with her. She then discovered that Mavis, her late mother's car, had a flat tyre. Already running late, she phoned Enzo.

'May I use your car? Mavis has got a flat and I haven't got time to change it.'

'Matteo can drive you. He's the best driver on my staff,' Enzo advised calmly.

'I'll change the tyre when we get back, *Signora*,' Matteo declared helpfully as she climbed into the SUV.

They were heading downhill into town when Matteo bit out something in anxious Italian. The big vehicle was jolting from side to side as the older man worked down through the gears. 'The brakes have gone!'

As they headed for a T-junction, Skye gripped the side of the seat as Matteo struggled to slow the car down and finally steered into the ditch.

'She's likely to tip over!' he warned her.

Her heart was in her mouth. There was a thunderous crash and the car juddered violently as it tipped into the ditch. She struck her head hard on the passenger window. Pain lanced through her temples and then blackness engulfed her and she knew no more...

CHAPTER TEN

SKYE WOKE SLOWLY. Her head hurt. She had the vaguest recollection of being sick, of medical staff fussing around her. Eyes opening in dismay, she started to sit up, realising that she was in bed, but her head swam so dizzily she flopped down flat again, struggling to overcome another bout of nausea.

'Thank goodness, you're back in the land of the living,' a familiar voice commented and she focused on her sister, who was standing beside the bed, clutching Shona on one hip. 'I came very close to strangling Enzo.'

'Why?' she whispered, stretching out her arms to her little sister, who was trying to break free of Alana's hold to reach her. 'Give her to me.'

Shona subsided into a clinging heap by her side, tucked between the bed bars and Skye's slight body.

'Where's Brodie?'

'He's with Enzo.'

'What happened? The car crashed, didn't it?' she whispered.

Alana sat down by the bed and sighed. 'It tipped over. Matteo actually did a very good job of saving you on that hill but you bashed your head and then the airbags went off and bruised you. You arrived in an ambulance. Matteo was a bit shaken up but he was all right and he phoned Enzo from the scene.'

Relieved that the older man was not hurt and that someone had remembered to pick up Brodie from his playgroup, Skye whispered, 'What did Enzo do?'

'Where do you want me to start?' Alana groaned. 'When he got a speeding ticket on the way to the hospital and got a police escort with sirens? When he created a scene in A & E and they threatened to throw him out? Nobody does drama like Enzo. If you'd been dead, Enzo would have thrown himself off the top floor.'

'Currently, your husband is fully occupied dealing with the police enquiry into the accident,' an older man in a white coat told her cheerfully as a nurse joined them to run through routine checks.

The consultant told her that she'd had a CT scan while unconscious and ran through her symptoms with her before asking her questions to check that she wasn't suffering from any mental confusion. Those completed, he remarked that the nausea and dizziness would take time to recede and that it would be best for her to spend the night in the hospital and once she got home she was to rest for a few days to aid her recovery. He added with a straight face that he didn't believe that the services of the top neurosurgeon on standby in London would be required. Skye rolled her eyes and even that small facial movement hurt.

The nurse was plumping her pillows to help her sit up when Enzo appeared in the doorway, Brodie clinging to his hand. Enzo had lost his tie and his lean dark features were taut and unusually pale but his strained dark eyes lit up like golden flames when he saw her awake. Her little brother tore free and raced up to the bed, only to be restrained by Alana. 'Careful, Brodie,' she said. 'Skye has a sore head.'

'Oopsie,' Skye confirmed, touching her fingers to her head and her face.

'Oopsie.' Brodie calmed as Alana lifted Shona from her side.

'Kiss better?'

'Sì...' Enzo breathed, striding forward to lift Brodie up so that he could kiss his big sister. 'Gentle, now.'

'You've taken ten years off my life,' Enzo told her unsteadily, brilliant dark eyes welded to her bruised and swollen face. 'Most people come round quickly after a concussion but you didn't and I was afraid that you would go into a coma.'

'And end up eternally asleep like the Sleeping Beauty,' Alana interposed with a hint of amusement.

'But you know what it took to wake *her* up and your husband was more than equal to the challenge.'

'I'm fine, Enzo.'

'You are many things right now but fine is not one of them. The airbags deployed and bruised you up because you're so small. When I saw you lying on that trolley in the emergency department, you were so white and still…' Enzo shook his tousled dark head to shake free of that recollection and visibly swallowed hard.

'I'll take the children back to the house,' Alana announced.

'The nanny will be staying on until Skye has recovered.'

Skye frowned at Enzo. 'I'll be right as rain by tomorrow.'

'You'll have to take it easy for a few days and you can't do that looking after Brodie and Shona. For once, *I'm* going to look after *you*,' Enzo proclaimed. 'I'll work from home for the rest of the week.'

'That's not necessary,' Skye began.

'Let him. It'll make him feel better,' Alana whispered as she gave her pale sister a gentle hug. 'See you soon.'

Silence fell as the room emptied.

'A *neurosurgeon* on standby?' Skye questioned in disbelief.

Enzo stood his ground and straightened his broad

shoulders, not an ounce of embarrassment on his dark strong face. 'I was really worried about you.'

'What did the police want?'

'They want to check over the car. The arson at the factory has made them suspicious. It should have been me in that car,' he breathed tautly. 'I wish it had been.'

'Well, I don't. I'm grateful that you're all in one piece. Matteo did a great job coming down that hill. And amazingly, he stayed calm.'

'He was a special ops soldier when he was younger.'

'I'm sorry... I've messed up your whole day,' Skye murmured.

'Is that a joke?' Enzo asked tightly.

'No, of course it's not a joke. I know how busy you are right now. The last thing you needed was a—'

'A dead wife?' Enzo sliced in rawly. 'And it could have been *all* of you in that car!'

'Thankfully, it wasn't.'

'When I saw you lying there, I realised something very important. I almost lost you. The shock was good for me.' Enzo paced restively at the foot of the bed, his bronzed profile tense. 'We need to have a serious talk tomorrow.'

Skye swallowed thickly. 'About what?'

'About us...this marriage.' Enzo made a slashing motion with one lean hand in a gesture of frustration. A chilling quiver of alarm ran down her taut spine. 'I've made a hash of it and now I'm probably going to make an even bigger hash by breaking the rules…but this is not the moment to discuss all that.'

Rules? What rules? He insisted on staying with her and, try though she did to remain awake, she drifted off to sleep, only opening her eyes when a nurse came to do checks on her again and offer her something to eat.

'Go home, Enzo,' she urged then. 'You look exhausted. Have you even eaten since this morning?'

'I bought snacks in the cafeteria for Brodie and Alana.'

Her heart melted inside her chest because she was willing to bet that he had seen to everyone else's needs before his own. She knew how her self-proclaimed spoilt, selfish playboy operated and he was exactly the opposite of what he said he was. Her eyes stung like mad and she wanted to slap herself for getting so sentimental and overwhelmed by her emotions, but she couldn't help it when she loved him so much. And what did he intend to discuss about their marriage? *He* had broken the rules? *What* rules? Had he worked out that they had grown too close to easily separate? Did he feel the need to remind her that they were still on the road to an eventual divorce? Or, even worse, had she betrayed the strength of her own feelings?

'Why are you crying?' Enzo sprang out of his seat and settled down on the side of the bed.

'I'm not crying. I think it's just the aftermath of the accident, a bit of shock or whatever,' she framed jerkily. 'Just ignore me.'

A blunt forefinger traced the path of a tear down her cheek. 'I've never been able to ignore you. I did try at the beginning before I got in too deep.'

'Too deep?'

'We're not about to discuss that now. You're not fit,' Enzo asserted, vaulting upright again, glittering night-dark eyes locked to her troubled face. 'Get a good night's sleep and we'll talk tomorrow.'

'If you're planning to ditch me, do it now. I'm not that fragile!' Skye declared, squaring her slight shoulders.

Enzo surveyed her in wonderment. 'Why would I ditch you? You're my wife.' Revealingly, he hesitated for a moment before grudgingly adding the qualifier, 'Sort of my wife.'

'A sort of a wife isn't a real wife and we both know that,' Skye told him flatly, crushing down the jolt of pain that had pierced her when he'd chosen to be precise enough to make that distinction.

Enzo gave her an intense appraisal, something of his inner turmoil etched in his rigid features and the unalloyed darkness of his gaze. 'We'll talk tomorrow.'

He felt guilty about wanting out of their marriage, she thought wretchedly. He was afraid of hurting or upsetting her and was determined not to do so when she was in a hospital bed, banged up from an accident. Or maybe he was planning to return sooner to Italy and was worried about how that would affect her adoption plans for Brodie and Shona. Could his attitude to her change so quickly? Enzo wasn't moody but he was volatile. He wasn't used to restrictions either, she acknowledged ruefully, and there were few living situations more restricted than that of a married man with young children. Well, whatever his decision, she would take it on the chin and stay strong.

The next day, when she was being discharged, Skye dressed with care in the clothes that she had specified by text that Enzo bring with him when he collected her. Only her hand emerged from behind the bathroom door to reach for the bag.

'You don't need to bother with make-up,' Enzo told her from his side of the door.

Oh, yes, I do. She had been horrified by the reflection that had met her in the mirror first thing. Her hair was a birds' nest and her face was puffy, her eyes pink. She looked awful and thought it would hardly be surprising if Enzo had looked at her the night before and wondered what he was doing with her. Dressed, with her hair tamed and a little cosmetic magic applied, she at least looked presentable.

'I just want to get you home,' Enzo told her, tucking her with care into a brand-new SUV. 'I think you should go straight to bed.'

'I'm already fed up with lying in bed. I'm not dizzy or sick any more. Whatever you've got to say to me, just get it over with,' she urged tightly.

'Not in the car,' Enzo said stubbornly, lean brown hands flexing round the steering wheel. 'But I should mention that your ex may be behind the arson at the factory. Apparently, there's evidence that his car was parked nearby in the middle of the night. The police suspect that he has an axe to grind with me.'

'Oh, my word.' Skye covered her shaken face with spread hands.

'It's not your responsibility. Don't let him overshadow our lives. Put your ordeal with him behind you and don't look back.'

That was easier said than done, Skye reflected unhappily. Ritchie would never even have known of Enzo's existence had she not moved into his house and started working for him. Of course, she felt guilty.

The house was unusually quiet. 'Where are the children?'

'Isabel took the kids to that indoor playpark in town.'

Equipped with a cup of coffee, Skye sat down in the sitting room. Enzo hovered restlessly by the door. For a moment she simply feasted her eyes on him, the lean, strong face with the classic features that had mesmerised her from their very first meeting. Sexual awareness lurched low in her body and she was embarrassed by her susceptibility. She couldn't ever look at Enzo without thinking of how it felt when he kissed her and touched her or without noticing how the energy in the room flared in his high-wire presence.

'I'll keep it brief,' Enzo promised tautly. 'When I first mentioned marriage to you, I attached a lot of absurd conditions to the agreement but everything's changed—at least for me, it has. I want to keep you.'

Her brow indented. 'As in…?'

'I want it to be a proper marriage. I want us to be permanent.'

Skye swallowed with difficulty. *Permanent?* Her lilac eyes flew wide in her heart-shaped face because she was stunned by that announcement. 'But—'

'Obviously I'm in love with you. *Crazy* in love with you,' Enzo breathed in a roughened undertone, spreading his hands wide in emphasis. 'Everyone else saw it but me. I didn't realise. I didn't get it. I didn't understand why I couldn't wait to get back here to you and the children every night. I honestly believed I wouldn't ever fall for anyone again and then it happened without me registering it.' He winced at that acknowledgement.

'*Crazy* in love with me?' Skye repeated with an arrested expression on her flushed face.

'Perhaps I'm not very attuned to what goes on in my head when it comes to the emotional stuff. At the beginning, I genuinely believed that I only wanted to help you, but the more time I spent with you, the more I wanted you, the more I liked you and the more reasons I found to keep us together.'

Skye nodded with a dreamy smile now starting to dispel the once tense line of her mouth. 'So, my engagement ring isn't only window dressing?'

'No. I wanted a ring on your finger, a ring that told everyone that you were mine, but I didn't want to admit that because it went against the rules I set at the start. We were supposed to be like friends with benefits, practical, unemotional, no attachment.'

'You picked the wrong girl. I'm seriously attached to you,' Skye admitted chokily, the turmoil of her roused emotions bringing tears to her eyes. 'I was so scared of getting hurt but I couldn't stop myself feeling more and more for you every day…and when we were in the Maldives, well…' Skye plucked at her dress and evaded his gaze. 'You made me feel *so* special—'

'Are you saying you love me too?'

Skye rose from her seat and closed both arms round him. 'I was scared of losing you. I thought maybe you were panicking and you'd taken on too much with us all and that you wanted out of our marriage again. And last night you said we had to have a serious talk about us! How much sleep do you think I got after that?' She struck his shoulder weakly with her fist in punishment for that sleepless night. 'Sometimes you don't think stuff through, Enzo. Of course

I assumed it was something bad and that I was going to lose you.'

'Always such a pessimist. You couldn't lose me if you tried. I will always be here for you. I have never felt like this before, so committed to one person that sometimes it's a struggle to stand you being out of my sight,' he confessed ruefully. 'I don't ever want to let you go. When you got hurt yesterday, it felt like my world had come crashing down. I attempted to picture my life without you and I *couldn't*.'

'But I'm OK,' she reminded him firmly, hands straying inside his jacket to the warmth of his chest, lingering over the muscles indented there, revelling in the warmth. And now she finally felt as though she had a proper right to touch him, to make her own moves without fear of what she might be revealing. 'I love you so much and tonight, I'm going to show you—'

Lining his fingers with hers, Enzo walked her towards the stairs. 'I'm out of bounds until you get medical clearance.'

'You can forget that. The way I see it, I got medical clearance the moment I left the hospital and this is a very special day and, right now, we're alone in the house.'

'Skye, I love you, but—'

'No buts. I don't want to wait until tonight.' On the landing, she kissed him with all the passion she had often tried to tone down.

Enzo lifted her off her feet with a groan. 'This is why I love you. You're stubborn and fiery and you stand up to me, so I suppose I have to compromise.'

'Compromise will be *so* worth your while,' Skye told him sunnily.

A wicked grin slashed Enzo's wide sensual mouth as he settled her down on their bed. 'You're mine now,' he said thickly.

Skye yanked him down on the bed by the edge of his jacket. 'You're mine too.'

Enzo doffed his jacket with enthusiasm and embarked on his shirt buttons. Skye shimmied out of her stretchy dress and he tugged her into his possessive arms and held her tight. 'I've got you.'

Skye buried her head in his shoulder, loving the smell of his skin and his hair, feeling like the luckiest woman in the world. He shifted lithely against her, acquainting her with his arousal, and excitement kindled. His lips connected with hers and the slow burn began in her pelvis, making her strain into even closer connection. And for a long time, there was mostly silence broken only by occasional gasps and sighs and mutterings until they both lay replete in each other's arms.

'I'll love you as long as I live,' Enzo swore hoarsely.

'So you have to live for ever.' Skye felt ecstatically happy for the first time ever, awash with emotion and hazy wonderful dreams of the future.

'Possibly a baby in a year or two?'

'Oh, definitely. Haven't Brodie and Shona turned you off in the slightest?'

'No, they taught me that I love having a family. We may move to Italy once the adoptions are finalised, but it's not set in stone,' Enzo murmured lazily. 'We'll see how we both feel when the time comes.'

EPILOGUE

SIX YEARS LATER, Skye twirled in front of the mirror in their bedroom. She had teamed a flimsy flirty skirt and a corset-type top in pale purple with sheer stockings and very high heels. It was Enzo's thirty-third birthday weekend. The evening before they had partied half the night away in an exclusive Roman club with their friends. But tonight, they were having a dinner party solely for two and she had given their staff the night off.

Donning a robe to cover the outfit because she didn't want the children asking tricky questions, she went to check on them. They lived in Tuscany in the midst of beautiful rolling countryside only a couple of miles from Enzo's grandparents and all the facilities of the town. Their home was an architect-designed contemporary house that was extremely spacious and comfortable. As soon as the adoption was granted, they had moved to Italy. Skye had wanted Brodie to have the time to become acclimatised to a new home and a new language before he started school. It had worked a treat because the children had initially picked up Italian much more easily than Skye, although she had since caught up.

Enzo had moved the headquarters of the Durante Group to Florence and now based himself there. That year when he had first become involved in running his vast inheritance had been a very busy one, incorporating loads of travel as Enzo acquainted himself with the different sections of the business. For a little while she had worried that he would turn into a workaholic, but her multiple pregnancy had immediately centred Enzo's interest on staying closer to home and spending time with the children they already had before the challenging birth of another three babies.

Luka and Gaetano looked at her with identical Enzo-style grins and abandoned their Lego fight to climb into bed without even being told. She tucked them in. They had madly curly black hair and Enzo's eyes and they were four years old. Next door their sister, Gianna, was already cuddled up with half her cuddly-toy collection in her princess bed. Gianna had green eyes like Alana and straight black hair she liked to wear in braids.

When Skye and Enzo had finally decided to try for a baby, they had assumed it would take a while for her to conceive. In fact, it had happened within weeks and they had both sunk deep into shock when they'd learned that Skye was carrying triplets. The pregnancy had been trying and the triplets had arrived early by C-section and now, with Brodie pushing nine and Shona seven years old, they had agreed that their family was complete.

Brodie was reading in bed. Brodie was always reading and quite the swot at school. 'I'm nearly finished, Mum,' he mumbled absently, barely looking at her.

Her little brother had asked her and Enzo if he could call them Mum and Dad after he started school. He understood that he was Skye's brother and he knew all about his late parents but, like many children, he didn't want to be different from his peers.

Resisting the urge to laugh at his uninterest, Skye went in to see Shona, who was a very pretty little girl but a complete tomboy, who modelled her wardrobe on her brothers. 'Is Dad home yet?' she asked sleepily.

'Not yet.'

Removing the robe and giving herself a last check in the mirror, Skye was heading downstairs when she heard Enzo's car and she smiled. Enzo strode through the door, complaining about roadworks and hold-ups while fending off Sparky's bouncy enthusiasm. Age had yet to slow Sparky down. 'Dinner awaits,' she told him.

As she served his favourite meal, which his grandmother had taught her how to cook, she was thinking about how happy she was. They saw a lot of Eduardo and Sophie Martelli, who had become as much Skye's family as they were Enzo's. Her relationship with Enzo and her self-esteem had gone from strength to strength after Ritchie had been found guilty and imprisoned. Once the arson attack, his part in it and his photograph had appeared in the newspapers, a couple of women had come forward to identify him to the police for assaulting them. But before those charges could even come to court, Ritchie had been killed in a prison riot.

Skye hadn't wished her ex-boyfriend dead, yet there was no denying that knowing he was no longer around gave her a certain sense of relief because she was convinced that while they were getting married in Italy, in an attempt to kill or seriously injure Enzo, Ritchie had cut the brake line on the SUV that had crashed. Regrettably, however, the police had been unable to find enough evidence to charge him with that crime.

'That's some outfit,' Enzo commented as their wine was poured, wondering what she was up to because Skye generally wore classic fashion and there was nothing conservative about what she was wearing. The provocative garments clung to her every delicate curve and showed off her shapely legs. He settled back to enjoy his meal, dark eyes lingering on her with appreciation. Skye always liked to keep him guessing.

'If only you knew,' Skye teased with a secretive smile.

'When do I get my surprise?'

'After dinner when we go upstairs.'

Anticipation infiltrated Enzo and he ate fast. He had never stopped being grateful for having met Skye and her siblings in his twenty-seventh year. She had turned his life around, smoothed his reconciliation with his grandparents and given him five fabulous children. He knew he had been rewarded five times over for stopping to help her that night on the road.

'Go lie on the bed. Get comfortable,' Skye instructed him tautly as she locked the bedroom door behind her.

He raised a brow, removed his jacket, tie and shoes and reclined back in relaxed mode against the carved headboard.

'If you laugh, I'll kill you,' she warned him anxiously before disappearing into her spacious dressing room. Music sounded, and it wasn't her usual style either. 'Pour Some Sugar on Me' by Def Leppard filled the room with a loud, raunchy rock beat.

And then Skye reappeared and began to dance, a little jerkily at first because she was visibly nervous. She needn't have worried because Enzo was transfixed from her first movement. It was the very last thing he had expected. In fact, he had been expecting her to produce another present from the dressing room. His jaw almost dropped when she tugged at her top and it detached from her body and went flying off. It was a specially made stripper outfit, he realised as the pouting curves he adored were bared, revealing glittery pink nipple pasties with tassels attached. He adored the surprise because Skye, being naturally shy about her body, had moved out of her comfort zone purely for *his* benefit.

As the music clicked off, Skye was in the act of crawling across the bed and he grinned at her, loving her so much in that moment for the anxious light in her eyes.

'Best present ever,' Enzo growled, lifting her up onto him, shamelessly acquainting her with the hard, urgent thrust of his arousal.

'Was it?'

'How did you learn to dance like that?'

'Videos online. Do you remember once asking me when I was going to rip my clothes off for your benefit?' she prompted eagerly.

'And you said *never…*' A heartbreaking smile curved his wide sensual mouth as he laced long fingers into her curls. 'I have never loved you more than at this moment and it was the sexiest show I ever saw because it was specifically choreographed for me.'

'I was scared you'd laugh,' she confided.

He kissed her with devastating passion until she was breathless. 'Never felt less like laughing. Much more in the mood for ravishing, *piccolo mio.*'

Skye beamed down at him, her insecurities vanquished, and her confidence restored because the smouldering glow in his dark golden eyes convinced her. 'I'm still crazy about you, Enzo.'

Enzo swung her down beside him and groaned. 'I'm besotted and sometimes I can't believe you're mine. We *have* to make the most of tonight because Alana is arriving on Monday and I'll be lucky to get five minutes with you for the first few days. You'll be gossiping morning, noon and night.'

'Yes,' she agreed sunnily as questing fingers played with the edge of her thong panties, and she gave an encouraging wriggle.

Before very long there was no further conversation and she lay afterwards in the circle of his arms, replete with joy and fulfilment.

* * * * *

If you fell in love with
The Maid Married to the Billionaire
*then make sure you catch the next instalment
in the Cinderella Sisters for Billionaires duet,
coming soon!*

*In the meantime, why not get lost
in these other stories by Lynne Graham?*

Promoted to the Greek's Wife
The Heirs His Housekeeper Carried
The King's Christmas Heir
The Italian's Bride Worth Billions
The Baby the Desert King Must Claim

Available now!

#4129 INNOCENT'S WEDDING DAY WITH THE ITALIAN
by Michelle Smart

Discovering that her billionaire fiancé, Enzo, will receive her inheritance if they wed, Rebecca leaves him at the altar and gives him twenty-four hours to explain himself. He vows his feelings are real, but dare Rebecca believe him and succumb to a passionate wedding night?

#4130 THE HOUSEKEEPER'S ONE-NIGHT BABY
by Sharon Kendrick

Letting someone close goes against Niccolò Macario's every instinct. When he receives news that shy housekeeper Lizzie Bailey, the woman he spent one scorching night with, is pregnant, Niccolò is floored—because his only thought is to find her and claim his child!

#4131 BACK TO CLAIM HIS CROWN
Innocent Royal Runaways
by Natalie Anderson

When Crown Prince Lucian returns from the dead to reclaim his throne, he stops his usurper's wedding, creating a media frenzy! He's honor-bound to provide jilted Princess Zara with shelter, and the chemistry between the ruthless royal and the virgin princess sparks an urgent, irresistible desire...

#4132 THE DESERT KING'S KIDNAPPED VIRGIN
Innocent Stolen Brides
by Caitlin Crews

When Hope Cartwright is kidnapped from her convenient wedding, she's sure she should feel outraged. But whisked away by Cyrus Ashkan, the sheikh she's been promised to from birth, Hope feels something *far* more dangerous—desire.

HPCNMRA0723

#4133 A SON HIDDEN FROM THE SICILIAN
by Lorraine Hall

Wary of billionaire Lorenzo Parisi's notorious reputation, Brianna Andersen vowed to protect her baby by keeping him a secret. Now the Sicilian knows the truth, and he's determined to be a father! As their blazing chemistry reignites, Brianna must admit the real risk may be to her heart...

#4134 HER FORBIDDEN AWAKENING IN GREECE
The Secret Twin Sisters
by Kim Lawrence

Nanny Rose Hill is surprised when irresistible CEO Zac Adamos personally proposes a job for her in Greece looking after his godson! She can't let herself get too close, but can the innocent really walk away without exploring the unforeseen passion Zac has awakened inside her?

#4135 THEIR DIAMOND RING RUSE
by Bella Mason

Self-made billionaire Julian Ford needs to secure funding from a group of traditional investors. His solution: an engagement to an heiress, and Lily Barnes-Shah fits the bill perfectly! Until their mutual chemistry makes Julian crave something outside the bounds of their temporary agreement...

#4136 HER CONVENIENT VOW TO THE BILLIONAIRE
by Jane Holland

When Sabrina Templeton returns to the orphanage from her childhood to stop her former sweetheart from tearing it down, playboy CEO Rafael Romano offers a shocking compromise... He'll hand it over if Sabrina becomes his convenient bride!

HARLEQUIN
PLUS

Try the best multimedia subscription service for romance readers like you!

Read, Watch and Play.

Experience the easiest way to get the romance content you crave.

Start your **FREE TRIAL** at
<u>www.harlequinplus.com/freetrial</u>.